A
Whole Lot
of
Lucky

A Whole Lot of Lucky

Danette Haworth

WALKER & COMPANY NEW YORK

First published in the United States of America in September 2012
by Walker Publishing Company, Inc., a division of Bloomsbury Publishing, Inc.
www.bloomsburykids.com

For information about permission to reproduce selections from this book, write to
Permissions, Walker BFYR, 175 Fifth Avenue, New York, New York 10010

Library of Congress Cataloging-in-Publication Data
Haworth, Danette.
A whole lot of lucky / Danette Haworth.
        p.   cm.
Summary: When twelve-year-old Hailee's family wins the lottery, her life changes in
unexpected—and not always good—ways.
ISBN 978-0-8027-2393-2 (hardcover)
[1. Best friends—Fiction. 2. Friendship—Fiction. 3. Moving, Household—Fiction.
4. Middle schools—Fiction. 5. Schools—Fiction. 6. Lotteries—Fiction. 7. Family
life—Florida—Fiction. 8. Florida—Fiction.] I. Title.
PZ7.H31365Who 2012   [Fic]—dc23   2011052331

Book design by Regina Roff
Typeset by Westchester Book Composition
Printed in the U.S.A. by Quad/Graphics, Fairfield, Pennsylvania
2 4 6 8 10 9 7 5 3 1

*For Michelle, and all the adventures we had
that Mom still doesn't know about*

A Whole Lot of Lucky

Chapter 1

. . . .

I didn't do it.

I am innocent.

I know convicts say that even when they're guilty, but I'm telling you the truth. At 3:05 today, I didn't mean to push Amanda on her bike so hard that she sailed off the curb and fell splat on the road in the pickup line after school. Thank God Mrs. McCrory had just paid the garage to tune up her Honda. That van stops on a dime now (and hardly even came close to hitting Amanda).

If you're the type of person who judges people guilty instead of presuming them innocent, you should put this book down and walk away. Don't even look back. But if you're still reading this—and I know you are because there you are and here I am—then you're the type of person who likes to know the truth, and that's just what I'm going to tell you.

"How do you like my new bike?" Amanda had asked, running her fingers along the pink, thickly padded seat. "It's got twelve speeds." She'd made a special trip to my house Sunday afternoon. Her shiny blond hair was still pinned back on either side in her church barrettes, but she'd changed from her dress into capris and a green top. Usually, I rode to her house after church, so that's how I knew she was showing off. A new bike—it wasn't even her birthday.

I stepped out from the chilly shadow of the house into the warm brightness of the day. Florida sunshine is at its best in February. Your feet feel like blocks of ice in the morning, but your toes are sticking out of sandals by lunch. The air is light and sends ribbons of sunshine through your window, inviting you to come outside and play.

Amanda stood by me as I took in the glittery seat, the tangle of wires that allowed for speed and braking, and the rainbow-colored monkeys she'd already clipped to the spokes. The frame was pink and white with black lightning striking the sides. "Nice," I said. "Can I ride it?"

Her gaze flitted over to our garage. Bougainvillea vines crept up the outside of it and wove green tendrils through the fraying net of the basketball hoop. Huge bunches of purpley-pink explosions hid the thin white paint of the cinder blocks. Occasionally, Dad cut the branches with his hedge trimmers, but those vines ran wild at night, growing an extra foot for each one Dad lopped off.

My bike leaned inside the openmouthed garage.

"I don't know," Amanda said and glanced down at her new wheels. She wrapped her fists around the snow-white handgrips. "It *is* brand-new, you know."

Just for your information, that right there was a direct insult to my bike. Mom bought it for me at a garage sale last summer after talking the guy down to three dollars. *You can't beat three dollars,* she'd said when I complained about it being a boy's bike and tomato red, which is my least favorite color next to orange. When we got the bike home, it took me half a roll of duct tape to hold the stuffing in the seat.

Amanda's new touring bike and its wide chrome handlebars shone between us, a gleaming beacon of coolness. Compared to mine—well, let's face it, that would be like comparing Disney World to the carnival that sets up the same Tilt-a-Whirl and sorry old Scrambler every fall.

"I'll give you a dollar," I said, fingering the hem of my jean shorts.

She bit her bottom lip. Sunlight glanced off her cheekbone as she angled her face away from me. "A dollar and a pack of Smarties."

She probably thought she was driving a hard bargain. I found the dollar on the road today and Smarties aren't even my favorite.

"How far can I ride it?"

She scrunched her lips. Her answer would make or break the deal and she knew it. "The DeCamps' house and back."

The DeCamps' house—two blocks and one orange grove away. The girl who lived there was our age but went to a private school so we hardly ever saw her. I thought over the deal, stepped up to the bike, and pushed down on the seat.

Amanda whisked my hand away. Shrugging, she said, "Sorry."

I clucked my tongue and touched the handlebars just to annoy her. Two blocks and one orange grove. "Okay," I said and trudged into the house, returning with my payment.

As I got on the bike, she started jabbering.

"Be careful with it! Don't change any of the speeds. I know you're not used to hand brakes so don't pinch them and no skidding!"

I cocked my foot on the pedal and pushed off.

"Don't ride in the gravel!" she yelled. "Watch out for glass in the gutter! Stay on the right side of the road!" I swear, if I had my own phone, she'd be a bug in my ear, calling out more do's and don'ts.

My hair fluttered in the wind as I rode away from her and all her henpecking. Trees raised their limbs as if cheering me on. A squirrel peeked up from acorn hunting as I passed. This bike glided—unlike my bike, which rasped like a cat with a hairball while you pedaled, announcing your journey to everyone you passed.

I rode her brand-new, not-her-birthday bike straight down Crape Myrtle Road and I felt like a princess with all the shiny chrome and whatnot when I reached the corner the DeCamps live on. Everyone knows they're rich. Only rich kids go to private school. I'll bet Emily DeCamp gets a new bike whenever the old one looks dirty.

The DeCamps' lawn rolled over their property with thick crowded sprouts of shag carpet grass. Most of our February yards looked like straw, but the DeCamps' yard was green, green, green. The grass was so thick you had to step up to walk on it, but don't do it because it'll hold your footprint as evidence until Mrs. DeCamp sees what you've done and will probably yell at you.

It had taken me only a minute or so to ride this far. That's how good Amanda's bike was. The road ahead urged me on, flashing its shiny rocks at me and lying flat to make itself more appealing. The rays of the sun stroked my back and lit on my freckles, and boy, if the breeze wasn't fluttering honeysuckle breath right under my nose.

I regretted, for a moment, being an upright citizen.

I turned the handlebars and glimpsed Amanda, who watched me like a hawk from the distance.

"What happened to your old bike?" someone said.

"Aagh!" I was so startled that the front wheel jagged

against a rock, I lost my balance, and almost pitched off the bike. I glared at the source of the voice. Emily DeCamp, sitting all hoity-toity on the brick stairs of her front porch. Righting the bike, I said, "I didn't see you."

She pushed her glasses up her nose. "I didn't want you to see me."

I hadn't considered that.

She stared at me. "Your hair is auburn."

My right hand automatically smoothed my hair. "It's titian," I said. Like Nancy Drew's hair, starting with book twenty-five, *The Ghost of Blackwood Hall*.

Emily DeCamp blinked. Then she scribbled something into a composition book. Her dark springy hair fell in front of her as she wrote, like a curtain when the show is over.

"Well . . ." I paused, put one foot on the pedal. "Bye."

"Bye," she said, not looking up.

As I rode back, I couldn't enjoy the sight of the last few oranges holding on to their branches or the speed of the bike because Amanda's eyes held me in their green tractor beam. She grabbed the bike before I even got off it. "Did you fall back there?" she asked.

"No, I'm okay."

Her eyebrows knitted together as she inspected one side of the bike, then the other. "You dented the fender."

"No, I didn't!"

If you've ever seen a perfectly nice blue sky morph into dark, sobby rain clouds, then you know what

Amanda's face looked like right then. "You did, too," she said. "I saw you fall!"

"I didn't fall!"

"That dent wasn't there before."

"Well, I didn't do it." I leaned to see the damage, but she jerked the bike away from me. I said, "Pipe down." I'd heard that on an old TV show and used it whenever I could.

One corner of her mouth hitched up. Her eyes glistened. Well, who could blame her? It *was* a brand-new bike. Gently, I ran my hand over the rear fender and, yes, there was a dent, but there's no way I did it. Curling my fingers under the fender, I pushed the metal up as hard as I could.

"You're going to break it!" But she didn't stop me.

Pop! The fender snapped into shape.

Amanda gasped. She crouched beside me, rubbed the fender, and smiled. "You fixed it!"

"It wasn't broken."

She shrugged. Sliding onto the cushy seat, she gestured toward the rear wheel. "Come on," she said. "Ride on the pegs."

"I'll get my bike."

"No! Ride the pegs—I promise I'll go fast!" She twisted her hand around the grip, pretending to accelerate. "You can ride *your* bike later."

Well! I believe I was offended. I started to assemble my face into the correct features for the occasion, but then I said to myself, *Self, you know you want to ride that bike, so just get on it already*, and then I did.

Hoisting myself up, I planted my hands on Amanda's shoulders, and she shoved off. We were still whooping and laughing as we passed Emily DeCamp, whose face flitted up like a sparrow's, cocking her head at the noise.

★ ★ ★

Amanda showed me the chalk outline in the garage that marked the parking spot for her new bike. "If Matthew leaves his skateboard or his bat or any of his stuff in my spot, he's in big trouble."

Matthew was three years older than us—a ninth grader, *high school!*—and a slob who got away with everything. Amanda had to wash dishes, do laundry, and help with the dusting, but all Matthew did was mow the lawn on the riding lawn mower. Now I ask you, is that even a chore?

I will admit—and this is secret—but Matthew also took out the trash, trimmed the bushes, and washed the cars, so he wasn't really a big, fat slob, but Amanda is my very best friend and I have to be on her side. (Matthew's not even fat.)

Amanda rolled the bike exactly into the center of its parking spot and booted the kickstand. She blew pollen specks off the seat. She polished the chrome with the hem of her shirt. She squeezed the tires to see if they needed more air. She couldn't have pampered that bike more lovingly if it were a dog.

We took off our shoes at the back door. I loved their house. Their mom read decorating magazines and tore out pictures from them. *Inspiration*, she'd say. Then Amanda and I had to tell her what we liked about the room in the picture and what we didn't like and next thing you know, Mrs. Burns was painting or putting up wallpaper or some such.

Takes money to do that, my mom says whenever I try to make little suggestions to her for our house. *We don't have the kind of income Mr. and Mrs. Burns do.* Behind my back, Mom refers to Amanda's mom as "Lady Burns."

"Matt-*eew*!" Amanda called out as we passed her brother in the kitchen on our way to the stairs.

I followed behind just as Matthew hefted the milk onto the island while sticking an Oreo in his mouth. Pouring the milk, he turned as I was about to pass him. "Hey, Hailee," he said in chocolate letters.

You'd think I'd be used to his eyes—I saw Amanda's all day long—but the pure greenness of them shocked me every time.

"Hi." My gaze fell to the floor and I rushed up the stairs behind Amanda. You'll notice I didn't put an exclamation point after I said "*Hi*." That's because I said it very quickly and sort of quietly. Whenever he's nearby, my heart beats too fast, my words get stuck in my throat, and my arms and legs move like a robot's. Matthew plays baseball and *never* moves like a robot.

Safe in Amanda's bedroom, I sank into her beanbag, which spilled out to make room for my butt while hugging my shoulders.

Amanda threw open her closet. "Three days or two days?"

Sundays were when we decided what we were going to wear for the school week. Three days meant dresses on Monday, Tuesday, and Wednesday; two days meant dresses on Tuesday and Thursday.

I drummed my fingers on my knee. My favorite outfit was getting tight across the top; I once caught a boy staring at me *right there* when he thought I wouldn't notice, so I folded my arms in front so there wouldn't be anything for him to look at. "Two days," I said. "If I could borrow your denim skirt?"

"Hail-*ee* . . ."

"Come on." I lowered my chin and batted my eyelashes at her.

She groaned. "Not the puppy face!"

My big brown eyes got her every time. Curving my mouth into a smile, I aimed a sparkle right at her.

"Aagghhh!" She pretended to strangle herself. "But I'm wearing it Tuesday."

★   ★   ★

Let me tell you something about Palm Middle School. You have the popular people, who everyone else supposedly hates but secretly wishes they were one. Then you have the *almost* popular people. They're allowed to sit with the popular people—maybe they knew them before they were famous; maybe they're cousins—but they have no popularity of their own to speak of. If you saw one of them at Kmart or the mall, you wouldn't even care. Amanda and I call them sidekicks because all they do is laugh at the popular people's jokes and follow them around.

Going down the line, you have the sidekicks of the sidekicks, the smart kids, the funny kids, the normal people, the kids who dress all in black, band geeks, nerds, and losers. You can tell who you are by the way people treat you. When I'm with Amanda, I feel like a normal person.

Thursday morning, I paired Amanda's jean skirt with my silky white T-shirt Mom found at Goodwill with the tags *still on*. When I pulled the top over my head, it whispered against my skin, sliding down my back like soft cascades of fresh spring water.

I padded across the wood floor of my bedroom, making sure to step on all the creaky spots so Mom would know I was getting ready for school. Turning in front of my dresser, I gave my reflection a quick once-over. My new top shimmered with every movement. I stuck gold-colored hoops through my ears and stepped back to examine the finished look.

This is why I needed a full-length mirror; I could see from my waist up only. Still, that's what most people are looking at, so I continued my inspection. Front—good; side—good; other side—small brown mole on tip of ear, but outfit good. I turned all the way around and craned my neck to see my back, which you know is impossible, but I liked that particular reflection, glancing over my shoulder with my mouth a little open, so I made a mental note to use that pose later.

"Hurry up, Hailee!" Mom yelled from downstairs. "Pancakes are ready!"

I spun to see the front again.

"Hailee!"

I peered into the mirror. I laughed silently to see how I would look later talking with Amanda. I picked up a book and held it in the crook of my arm. I put the book down. I stared at myself as if I were a stranger and saw this girl in the mirror. My eyes fell to the waves of silk.

I stared a little harder.

Was that? . . . *Oh, no . . .* it was! I could see the faint outline of my first bra through the shirt.

"HAILEE!"

"MOM!" I stomped my foot at the same time. My fingers pulled at the fabric—maybe if the shirt lay differently—

"BREAKFAST!"

"I'LL BE RIGHT DOWN!" I rubbed off the top like a snake shedding skin and grabbed a wrinkled green T-shirt from my closet floor. On it, a bunny is looking at a frog who says, "Rabbit." I thought it was funny when I got it for Christmas in fifth grade. Now I was in middle school and I thought it was stupid, or I should say, I *discovered* it was stupid after a sidekick told me, "Hey, that's stupid." But you couldn't see through it, so I put it on.

Downstairs in the kitchen, Mom arched one penciled-in eyebrow at me. I have practiced that expression with Amanda, but the only way I can do it is if I hold the other eyebrow in place with my fingers.

"Sorry," I said in a rush and kissed the fuzz on my baby sister's head before sitting down.

"Aa-ee!" That's "Hailee" in baby language. Libby is one and a half years old. Olivia is her full name, which is why I call her Libby.

I tugged Libby's feet under the tray of her high chair and she squealed and stamped her baby fork on the tray.

Mom frowned at my shirt. "I thought you were wearing the new one today."

"Doesn't fit," I lied, shoveling the best blueberry pancakes ever made into my mouth.

"Well, you can't go to school in that one—it's wrinkled. I'll get a different top for you."

"No time!" I slurped my orange juice. "I'll be late!"

She glanced at the clock on the microwave, sighed,

and slid into the chair across from me with her coffee. Snuggling into Libby's face, Mom said, "Olivia was a good newspaper girl today." She tickled her feet. "Yes, you were! Yes, you were!" That's all it took for Libby—she giggled, snorted, banged the high chair with her heels, and grabbed her cut-up pancake bits in her fists, squishing them through her fingers like Play-Doh.

Mom's newspaper route was fun. She drove through town with both windows open, pitching newspapers out both sides without even slowing down—her arm's that good. Sometimes I thought about getting up early to help her on Sundays, but I never did more than think about it. I'm not what you'd call a morning person—at least, not a *four o'clock*-in-the-morning person.

I glanced at the back door. Dad's work sneakers were gone. "Did Dad have an early job today?" I asked between blueberry bites. Dad cleans carpets—that's his business and he is the owner and also the only employee. The good thing about Dad's business is we have the cleanest carpet in town. The bad thing about Dad's business is that his customers all live around here, which means he's like a servant in the houses of my classmates.

Mom set her cup down. "Three, actually—in Hill Crest." Hill Crest is the la-di-da gated community across town. Once when Libby was sick and Mom had to take her to the doctor, Dad brought me with him to a job there. Talk about security! Not only is there a gate, there's a security guard, video cameras, and signs telling you about the guard and cameras. I never saw a neighborhood so stuck on itself. Past the gate, you can hardly believe your eyes. Those aren't houses—they're mansions, and that means a lot of carpet to clean and maybe even sofas and drapes.

I swirled the back of my fork through the leftover syrup on my plate, licked it off, and then cleared the table. The phone rang. Mom and I groaned at the same time. Since I happened to be standing by the sink, I answered it after looking at the caller ID. "Hi, Mrs. Gardner, how're you today?"

"I'd be a lot better if I got my paper."

Cranky old lady. Her voice sounded like crushed aluminum foil. One of her grandsons was in my math class. "Hang on," I said. "Here's my mom."

Mom rolled her eyes and shook her head as she reached for the phone, but not before giving me a quick hug. Poor Mom. You'd think when you're an adult you'd be done with getting in trouble.

Speaking of trouble, as I rode up to the bike area outside the school, there they stood, Megan and Drew, leaning against the light post. They were on me like mosquitoes.

"Really?" Megan said in that superior voice of hers. "Wearing a skirt on *that* bike?"

"Oh, my God," Drew said, and they laughed.

Becca Singer shot me a look of sympathy before she scooted out of target range.

Heat crawled up my neck, but I walked on by. They followed me into the pen and I pretended like they weren't there, which was supposed to discourage them but never did. I took a deep breath and bent down to lock up my bike.

Megan's feet pranced closer to me. "You're wearing Amanda's skirt!"

I whirled around. "No, I'm not!"

"You're right—she is!" Drew said to Megan.

I stood and threw my fists down, arms rigid at my side. "I am not!"

Megan started laughing and turned to Drew. "The A—"

"A for Amanda! You did it when we dressed out at gym!" Drew cracked up too much to say anything else.

I couldn't help it; I glanced at the skirt but didn't see anything. Then, feeling better, I smoothed the skirt down the seams and that's when I spotted it: a spiky red A inked in near the hem. Pings of heat fired off all over my face, even in my eyeballs.

Megan put one hand on her hip. "Told ya!"

"The least she could do is wash things before she wears them," Drew said.

Megan threw her head back with a wide-open laugh.

Somewhere between elementary school and middle school, Megan got popular. She's pretty but not super-pretty, though she does wear cool clothes and I guarantee they're not from picked-over bins at the thrift store. She's

not the smartest or the fastest or the funniest, and she's
definitely not the nicest. How does a person like that get
to be popular? Let me know if you figure it out, because
I sure haven't.

Megan linked her arm through Drew's and they
strolled away, sniggering.

A couple of other kids overheard everything. From
the sides of their eyes, they searched for the red A. Instead
of slinging my backpack onto my shoulder, I let it hang
from my elbow. The heavy books inside banged against
my thigh as I marched past the rubberneckers, but there
was no way I was walking around with Megan's A for
all to see.

I searched the sidewalk and then the courtyard for
Amanda. The first bell rang, which had the same effect
as a traffic light turning yellow. Some people sped up,
but others screeched to a stop. These would be your
popular people. They thought they owned the halls,
standing in circles, forcing the rest of us to flow around
them. I squeezed past the first blockage, got pushed
against a locker, then picked up by the current, which
floated me down the hall and deposited me at my first-
period classroom: social studies.

Amanda sat at a desk with her legs crossed, pretending to look for something in her folder. This is a tactic
we both used when we didn't have anyone to talk with
and didn't want to look like losers.

"Amanda," I said as I took the seat next to her,

"look." I tapped the side of the skirt and told her the whole story.

As I spoke, her shoulders sagged and her mouth pinched together like a clam's. She started shaking her foot. The more I talked, the harder that foot bounced. Finally, she said, "I told you I didn't want you borrowing my clothes anymore."

"You never said that!"

"Well, it should've been obvious," she said. "Besides, I didn't want to hurt your feelings."

My mouth dropped open.

"This is so embarrassing." She put her head on her desk. Her long blond hair slipped over the side in ropes.

Before I could say anything back, the tardy bell rang and Mrs. Weller called out roll.

Apparently, Megan and Drew texted everyone in their contact lists about their little trick, because all day long I thought I heard people whispering, "Hey," but what they were really saying was this: "Where's the A?" "I see the A!" Amanda gave me the silent treatment at lunch. Becca told me to hide it with duct tape. Tanner Law walked up to me and said, "Rabbit!"

By the time school was over, I was ready to disappear. Amanda came up behind me in the pen. I thought she was going to apologize, but instead she said, "Just keep the skirt, okay? I don't want it back." Her voice was flat.

"It's not *my* fault," I snapped.

"Whatever."

I watched as she unlocked her new twelve-speed bike with the Sure-Grip hand brakes and the butt-soft seat, and I watched as she daintily got on—daintily, because hers is a girl's bike—and I was still watching as she rode away and the back wheel slipped into the long crack between the concrete sections.

Megan, Drew, and their sidekicks pointed and snickered at her straining on the pedals. One of the lesser sidekicks slapped his knee as if Amanda stuck in a crack was the funniest thing he'd ever seen in his whole entire life. One of them took out her phone and I heard the words "video" and "YouTube" and "loser," and that's when I did it—that's when I sprinted toward Amanda and pushed her bike seat as hard as I could.

The back tire hopped out of the crack just as Amanda stood on the pedals. Her bike did a fierce wheelie, and she sailed over the curb into the pickup line. For a moment, it looked like she might right herself, like a jumper on a horse, but then her tires hit the pavement and she fell off in one direction and the bike fell in another. Mrs. McCrory jammed on her brakes hard enough to cause her van to buck.

A gasp from the entire car-pool lane sucked the air off the playground, through the dollar weeds, and over the vans trembling in line, causing a silence so sudden that the sandhill cranes who'd been foraging nearby straightened their long gray necks and turned disinterestedly in our direction.

Mrs. McCrory hopped out of her van, her face pale white. "Thank God I just had the brakes fixed!" she said, fanning herself with her hands.

I started toward my best friend when suddenly one of the teachers yanked my arm and dragged me to the middle of the crowd, where Amanda sat on the road being petted and murmured over. The teacher sliced through the air for quiet. She asked, "Is this the girl who pushed you?"

Amanda's face was red. Her knee was scraped. She was breathing so hard her nostrils flared like a bull's before it charges. She locked her eyes on to mine and I saw in them a stony glint I'd never seen before.

"Yes," she said through gritted teeth. She shifted into a more solid position. "That's her."

Chapter 2

· · · · · · · · · · · · · ·

Teachers say they try to be fair. But if you are in at least fourth grade, you already know that's not true. None of the teachers even tried to listen to my side of the story. And Amanda didn't help one bit, not one single bit. She glared at me as they practically slapped cuffs on my wrists and dragged me to the office of the warden, Principal Dr. Taylor, which is how I ended up sitting here in the lobby, waiting, staring at gobs of gum stuck under the receptionist's desk and counting floor tiles (sixty-eight).

I've almost given up hope of ever seeing the outside again when the principal herself comes out to get me.

"Hailee Richardson," Dr. Taylor says as she ushers me into her office. She sits on her throne behind the desk; I sit on a hard plastic chair. She tilts her head and says, "We've never had behavior problems with you before. What brings you here today?"

Never before have I sat in this office. It's nothing like I imagined. Instead of paddles hanging from hooks ready to discipline troublesome students, fancy diplomas decorate the walls. The plant on her desk is *not* a Venus flytrap like I've heard, but an African violet. Classical music plays softly through her computer speakers.

Still, when I look at her, I see the piercing eyes of an eagle. I fold my hands together and squeeze them. "Is my mom coming?"

Dr. Taylor leans against her high-back velvety chair. A container of half-eaten Chinese food with a plastic fork sticking out of it lies in her trash can. Everyone knows you're supposed to use chopsticks when eating Chinese (though I do use a fork myself, but you'd expect an adult to do things the right way). "I called your mother. She and I had a nice chat over the phone."

Oh, no.

"So," she says, shifting forward in her seat, "what happened in the car lane?"

The principal called my mom. I'm going to be in so much trouble. My eyes fill with tears.

"Hailee?"

A soft knock interrupts her, and we both turn and see in the doorway the clinic nurse and Amanda, whose knee has a big square bandage on it. "Just a scrape," the nurse says and pats Amanda's back. "She'll live."

A smile almost sneaks across my lips, but the daggers shooting from Amanda's eyes pin my mouth in place.

She crosses her arms and stands in the doorway even after the nurse leaves.

"Come in and sit down," Dr. Taylor says.

Amanda scoots the other plastic chair far away from mine, then settles into it with a huff.

Dr. Taylor nods to Amanda. "Why don't you tell me what happened?"

"She pushed me! Right into the cars!"

"That's not what happened!"

"Yes, it is!"

Panic leaps in my heart. Why is Amanda saying that? I could get suspended or expelled or even sent to juvie, where girls file toothbrushes into knives and stab each other. I glance from Amanda to the principal. "I didn't push her into the road; I pushed her out of a crack." My lips quiver as words find their way to my mouth. "Amanda's tire was stuck. I was trying to get her out of the crack because Megan and Drew were laughing at her."

"Megan and Drew," Dr. Taylor says. She taps her lips with her fingers.

Amanda twists in her seat and asks in a small voice, "They were laughing at me?"

"They were *recording* you."

Dr. Taylor *tsks* disapprovingly.

I say, "They're always making fun of people. They call Sara Lardiss, 'Sara Lard A—'" I stop right there before a swear word comes tumbling out. "Just because she's"—I stumble for how to say this—"a little over-weight, they call her names. And they're the ones who threw meatballs at the lunch lady last week, and look what they did to my skirt." I pull the hem out to show her.

"They ruined that skirt," Amanda says.

Dr. Taylor cranes her neck to see the damage. Then, nodding to herself, she says, "Those are all important things, Hailee, but we need to get to the bottom of what happened today with *you*. The teachers saw you push Amanda into the road—"

"She was trying to help me." Amanda sits up straight. "It's *my* fault I lost my balance. Please don't get her in trouble." She lifts her knee. "It doesn't even hurt."

Drumming her pencil on her desk, Dr. Taylor's piercing eagle eyes dissolve into regular human eyes. "Girls, I think what we have here is a misunderstand-ing." She points her pencil at Amanda. "Your bike was stuck." Amanda's whole body nods in response. The pencil points at me. "And you were pushing the bike out."

"Yes."

She exhales loudly. "Go home, girls. Watch out for cracks and look both ways." She closes a manila folder. Amanda and I stand up and begin to leave. I rise like a helium balloon, free and light, ready to float out of there until Dr. Taylor stops my escape.

"Hailee?"

I freeze.

"Maybe you're stronger than you realize."

She makes me sound like a bodybuilder. Her piercing eagle eyes return. "Keep it in check, okay?" Then she promises to call my mom and explain what happened.

Outside at the bike rack, Amanda says, "Thanks for sticking up for me."

"Thanks for sticking up for *me*," I say back. It takes a second, just long enough to swing my leg over the boy bar of my bike, for me to realize there's a little hurt worming its way through my heart. "Why would you think I pushed you into the road?"

She fumbles with her handlebars. "I don't know. I just . . . um . . ."

"What?"

She lifts her eyes to me and shrugs one shoulder. "I thought you were jealous of my bike."

Well! A strange mix of feelings hits my stomach.

"I'm sorry," she says, "and I really do want you to keep the skirt because I know how much you like it." She smiles. My stomach churns and my head fills with heat. She cocks a pedal. "Want to come over to my house?"

I wouldn't be jealous in a hundred million years.

"Hailee, what's the matter? Are you mad?"

I am not mad. I am not jealous. I am just leaving. My body moves on its own, toes pushing against the sidewalk for a kick-start, feet hitting the pedals. I ride past her and keep going.

"Hailee! I said I was sorry!"

Past the playground, past the field, up to the crossroad where I go left and she has to go right. I don't even stop at the sign.

"Hailee!" Her voice is at the crossroad. "I was wrong, okay? I said I was sorry! I was wrong!"

My pedals churn like my stomach. The chain rattles, whining higher and higher the faster I go. The whole bike frame squeaks and grates; the loose chain guard rasps against the links.

I hate shopping at thrift stores, I hate not having my own phone, and I hate that my mom delivers newspapers to people I go to school with.

My rear tire pelts me with gravel.

I hate this bike.

Chapter 3

. . . .

The afternoon is sour as grapefruit, which no one really likes but everyone eats when they're on a diet. Mom bangs cupboard doors shut and raises the cleaver high as she chops the heads off broccoli. "A phone call from the principal!" *Whack!* "The principal, Hailee!" *Whack, whack!* "Wait till your dad hears about this!" One final whack, then she pushes the severed broccoli heads into a pot of boiling water.

I plan to serve as my own lawyer. Though my mom has the position of mother behind her, I have the testimony of the principal. That, and the fact that Amanda admitted her knee didn't even hurt. Just look at all the trouble I've gotten into over nothing.

Mom stops clanging around for a second. "Are you even listening to me? This is important."

For Mom, school is almost as important as church.

She barely graduated. Whenever she tried to read her textbooks, the letters would trick her and change places. So if she was trying to get through a sentence that read, *Put nuts in the pan for a nice tang*, my mom would see, *Put stun in the nap for a nice gnat*. That kind of reading put her in the lower classes, and even there she got bad grades. In math, too, because numbers know how to jump around just as well as letters do.

It wasn't till after high school that she heard of dyslexia, which is the medical word for the way her brain mixes up the letters and numbers. By then, she was on her own and paying her rent by working as a waitress. That's how she met my dad.

I flick a Cheerio across Libby's tray and she chases it with her hand.

"Yes, I'm listening to you," I say, making a Cheerio tower. Libby knocks it down and eats the pieces.

"You've got to take these things seriously."

My honor roll ribbons flutter as Mom opens the refrigerator for ingredients. A handprint I painted in third grade is held to the freezer part with magnets. I used fluorescent paint and silver glitter and filled every square inch with color. Even though the corners are curling, Mom keeps it up there. She thinks it's pretty.

"Mom?"

She lays down the cleaver. "Yes?"

"I need a new bike." I push Libby's Cheerios around so I don't have to see Mom's reaction.

At first, she doesn't say a thing, just picks up the cleaver and starts chopping again. Then, in an even voice, she says, "We need a lot of things around here. Go upstairs and do your homework."

I didn't have my snack yet, but I know better than to argue with her after hearing that tone of voice.

My pale pink walls don't cheer me up as much as they usually do. I toss my backpack to the floor and lie on my bed, staring at the popcorn ceiling and the one cobweb in the corner I keep forgetting to knock down. The more I don't clean it up, the worse it gets. It's grown an extra tentacle since the weekend.

Below it, my memo board is so loaded with pictures, you can't even see the quilted purple fabric underneath. When I get new pictures, I stick them right over the old ones. Sometimes, I pick a spot and slide off the top picture, and then the next, and then the next one after that. It's like going back through time. There's even a picture of Amanda and me in diapers, playing together. I keep that one buried, but I know exactly where it is.

I hate being in fights with people. Today I've had three: Amanda, Mom, and you have to count my dad, too, because in about two hours, he's going to hear all about it.

I roll onto my side. The swamp maple that's as tall as our house waves its cheery red leaves at me. The branches stretch across my window, sometimes holding a squirrel or a bird for me to get a good, up-close look. People always talk about fall colors—that's a northern idea. Sometimes, the truth of a thing depends on where you're looking at it from. For instance, in Florida, red leaves pop from our maples around Valentine's Day. I ask you, could that be any more perfect?

Also, birds don't fly south for the winter; they fly north for the summer. This has nothing to do with my cheery maple, but I just thought I'd mention it.

★   ★   ★

Mom shouts from downstairs she's taking Libby out in the stroller. Her voice has forgotten she was mad at me. Still, I answer back without opening my door.

I've finished my decimal multiplication homework. I read chapter twenty-three in social studies. I answered questions one through thirty (odd numbers only) in science. All that's left is PE, which of course there's no homework for; language arts; and Family Science, which is really home ec but they changed the name so it wouldn't sound old-fashioned and so boys would take it.

As I wrangle with my backpack trying to fit everything back in, a shred of lined notebook paper floats out. I know what it is without looking, but I pick it up anyway. Amanda's bubblegum print, fat and happy with hearts over the i's. *Can you still spend the night Friday? My mom will get doughnuts!*

I've spent so many Friday nights at her house that I

don't remember which one this note is talking about, but when I read the words, I hear Amanda's voice in my head. I would like to point out, before I go any further, that I had been thinking about Amanda earlier, so it wasn't seeing the note that made me get the phone and punch in her number.

Her phone rings and rings and rings. I hang up and dial again. Then I hang up and block my number, but she still doesn't answer. I hit redial. Hang up. Redial. Hang up. Redial. Hang—

"Hailee!" Irritation scratches across the air waves and into my ear. "What are you doing?"

"Why didn't you answer?"

She huffs into the phone. "If you must know, I was in the bathroom."

Hmm. Well, I guess certain things can take a while in the bathroom. "Okay," I say.

She breathes into the phone, then asks, "Well?"

"Well, what?" I hadn't prepared a speech.

"Well, why did you call?" she asks. "Hurry up, too, because I've only got a couple of bars."

Liar. That's what she tells her grandma when she doesn't know what to say to her.

I look at the shred of notebook paper in my hand. "Are you still spending the night this Friday?"

Pause. "I didn't know you invited me."

"I just did."

Silence crackles between us. I didn't ask my mom

about this, but I know she'll say yes. She calls Amanda her adopted daughter.

Suddenly, my adopted sister erupts. "You ignored me! You heard me calling you—I take back my apology! I had the worst day today and it was all your fault!"

"*My* fault? You're the one who left your skirt out for Megan to write all over, and you're the one who didn't notice the A when you put it back on."

She's quiet, so I keep going. "You got me sent to the principal! My mom's mad at me, my dad's going to lecture me, and I'll never go to college now. So I think *I'm* the one with the worst day today, not you."

"It was just so embarrassing," she says. "All day long."

"I know—I was the one wearing the skirt!"

"Witches with a B," she says, and I know for a fact she's shaking her head at the thought of them.

"Yeah," I say, "witches with a B."

We snicker into the phone. I feel the connection reaching for five bars.

After checking with her mom, she says she can't spend the night because her aunt's coming over for the weekend. I'm disappointed, but when we hang up, I feel better than I did before I called. At supper, Dad asks me about my visit to the principal's as he passes the mashed potatoes. He puts on a stern face. Between you and me, I'm 100 percent positive Mom ordered him to lay down the law.

Dad listens to my side, says a few things that Mom nods her head to, then tells me to make sure it never happens again. He clears his plate. "I'm going out to cut back the vine," he says. "It's choking the gutter."

"Can I help?" I ask.

"You can hold the ladder."

Boring! I wanted to use the choppers. But I don't want Dad to fall, so I spend the next hour with my palms pressed against the aluminum rails while thorny arms of green and pink bougainvillea fall around me. Dad talks to it, scolding it for scratching him and telling it to stay out of the gutter. Some people think talking to plants makes them grow better. If that's true, Dad is only making his own life harder.

★   ★   ★

The next day at school, some girls come up to me and tell me how rotten I am for pushing Amanda into the car-pool lane, even though they can plainly see Amanda standing right next to me. I stick up for myself, but they turn their backs on me and cut into the stream of people rushing to class.

I don't ask her, but Amanda says, "I didn't know what to say."

Friday and Saturday are boring without her. When I call Becca on Saturday, she's not home, either. Becca sometimes eats lunch with us. She's not my best friend, but she wears alien ears to school and can speak Kling-on, which is a planet in the Star Trek series, so Amanda and I like her pretty much.

I get on my bike and think about the book I've been reading at night, *Because of Winn-Dixie*. Opal was lucky she found that dog at Winn-Dixie instead of say, Peri-odontics, which is some kind of dentist place. Of course, she probably would've shortened the name to Peri, so that wouldn't have been a problem because it's still cute.

I ride my bike up and down Crape Myrtle Road, trying to think of a gross business name that Winn-Dixie could have been stuck with. The notes of a flute drift from the second-story window of the DeCamps' house. So pretty and light, the notes fall like the cottony feathers of a dandelion. If I were friends with Emily, I would ask to sit on her front porch and listen to her flute playing and the birds, who are calling back to her.

Boring Saturday finally comes to an end. My sheets are cool and my room is dark and it feels good to snuggle in, all nice and cozy. I rub my feet against each other to warm them up. Big elephant ears of sleep layer over me. I'm slipping into dreamville.

Screams from downstairs shatter my ears awake. *Mom!* I jolt up in bed—heart pounding, blood surging—then I flip down and squeeze my eyes shut because robbers won't kill me if they think I'm sleeping, but Mom is still screaming and Dad is screaming *and* crying, and I say, "God!" because I'm too scared to say a longer prayer.

If I had my own phone, I could dial 911.

Tears slide down my face in torrents. My throat wells up in a painful ball. I lie there, crying and awaiting my fate until I hear my dad's low-throated chuckle, which gives way to whooping and hollering and honest-to-God, he goes right back to screaming and crying again.

I shove off my covers and tiptoe past Libby's room. She sleeps her baby sleep, oblivious to all the commotion below us. Annoyance creeps down the stairs with me as I make my way to the landing. Dad stands in front of the TV, dumbstruck, staring; Mom sits on the couch in her fuzzy green housecoat, rocking back and forth.

Their faces shine when they notice me. They glow like angels. Light pours out of their eyes and off their skin, and it scares me half to death.

I hear my voice tremble as I ask, "What's wrong?"

Dad's face screws up. He cries and grabs my hands. His mouth moves but no words come out.

"Hailee." Mom's voice is hoarse. Tears have wet her cheeks; crying has turned them red.

I'm afraid of whatever she's going to say next.

"Hailee," she croaks. "We just won the lottery!"

Chapter 4

. . . .

It can't be true.

I look from Mom to Dad and back to Mom. Something's happened, something that's turned them into crazy people.

"What are you talking about?" I ask.

Dad bear-hugs me, and my feet leave the ground. My legs flap like noodles. "We won! We won! We won the lottery!"

My brain's confused, sloshing around in my skull with all of Dad's jostling. Wriggling out of his arms, I drop my feet to the floor and go to my mother. I kneel in front of the nappy brown couch and peer into her eyes for signs of crazy. "Is he right?"

Mom stretches out her arms and puts both hands on my shoulders, including the one holding a used tissue, but I don't yank away because this is important. "Your dad," she starts, then dabs at her nose with the wet Kleenex. "Your dad *bought the winning ticket!*"

"NO WAY!" But I know it's YES WAY! I jump up and down, knocking into the table and spilling Mom's coffee on it, but who cares anyway because we can just buy a new one. "OHMYGOSH! WE WON THE LOTTERY!" My fists pump up and down. I hop on the couch and do a little jig, then jump off, grab Dad's hands, and whirl him around like ring-around-the-rosie. Flinging him across the room, I slide into some dance moves. "We're rich! We're rich! We're really, really rich!"

Then it hits me for real. I buzz in circles around the room screaming. Mom and Dad start laughing, then I start crying. Mom pulls me over to the couch and tries to nestle me, but power surges through my body. I pop up and do everything all over again, then yell, "I've got to call Amanda!"

I sprint to the phone, but Dad hooks me with his arm. "Hey, girlie," he says. "It's after midnight!"

"But, Dad!"

Mom rises from the couch. I slip my arms from Dad and windmill around the room. Mom ducks out of my way. "Dad's right, honey—it's too late to call someone's house. Besides"—she's talking to Dad now—"we might want to think about this before we start spreading the news."

"What's there to think about?" I break into

celebration again, dancing, pumping, running. It takes me a minute to realize I'm celebrating alone. Mom sets up the coffee machine, then joins Dad at the kitchen table, where they have their Serious Talks.

Let them talk. Let them drink coffee! We just won the lottery! "We're millionaires!" I shout and throw my arms high in victory.

Running upstairs to my room, I stop at Libby's door and tiptoe to her crib. She will not remember this night. She will not remember the night that changed her whole entire life before she even lived it. She will not remember, but I will tell her.

I stroke the top of her head, then her cheeks and her little eyebrows. "We're rich," I whisper, following the curve of her ear with my fingertips. She is softer than air. When we hire a nanny, I will make sure the nanny is soft, too. Maybe she could sing, like Mary Poppins.

Once in my room, I flop onto my bed with a notebook and a pencil. "Things I Need," I write at the top. Things I need come flying in from all corners of the room and I write fast to keep up:

1. New bicycle
2. Cell phone
3. New clothes (from where Megan and Drew shop)
4. Full-length mirror
5. TV for my room
6. DVD player for my TV

I glance around for the best place to put my new TV.

   7. TV stand

Then I take a hard look at my room. The bottom left drawer of my dresser gets stuck so hard, the only stuff I keep in it are things I never use. A coaster under one leg keeps my nightstand level. My headboard doesn't match.

   8. New furniture for my room

Oh! Oh!

   9. Computer

I sit back and think about this. A computer stays in the room. You can't take it downstairs or to your friend's house. I cross out *computer*.

   9. ~~Computer~~ Laptop

Yes, a laptop is better, because I could sit outside with it and do homework. But then again, laptops don't have as much memory as computers and what if it's raining outside?

I draw a line through *laptop* and stare out my window. My cheery red maple holds its pointy leaves in the moonlight, sending sharp shadows across my room. Soon, it will lose its red leaves and sprout green ones.

Laptop or computer. I can't make up my mind. Wait! Wait!

9. Computer

10. Laptop

See how easy being rich is?

★   ★   ★

"Remember," Mom says as we walk from the car to the church the next day, "don't tell anyone about You Know What."

She acts like we've won a head full of lice rather than a buttload of money.

One of Mom's church friends passes us, hurrying because she's in the choir. "Don't forget to stop at the pantry today," she says. "New bread from Tochino's."

"We probably don't need it," I say. We don't need the free day-old bread the restaurants donate to the church, even if it is Tochino's Garlicky Toast, which normally I take as many loaves as I can and Mom makes me put them all back except for one.

"Thanks, Lisa," Mom says. "We'll check it out." After Miss Lisa passes, Mom slides closer to me. "*What* did I tell you?"

"I didn't say anything about You Know What."

"Hailee—"

Dad swings an arm around my shoulders; his other arm carries Libby in her car seat. "All Hailee the queen, the *quiet* queen." He pulls me in. "Mom and I want this to be secret for a while, okay?"

Grown-up time is different from kid time, and it changes depending on the situation. For example, when you're stuck in the backseat of the van and the air conditioner isn't cold enough because your mom is always freezing and plus you're hungry but she won't stop at Burger King, and you ask, "How much longer will this take," every mom will say, "Oh, just a few more minutes." And those minutes turn into hours, which isn't just a few minutes but a lot.

Later, when your favorite show is on and it's almost to the point where something big is about to happen, your mom says, "Bedtime," and you say, "Just a few more minutes," and what you get is about *one* minute. Maybe two if you're lucky. So grown-up time is like dog years in that way.

The morning breeze blows words out of my mouth. "Millionaires," I whisper into it. "How long do we have to keep it secret?" I ask.

"I don't know," Dad says.

My hair flutters like kite ribbons around my face. They say March roars in like a lion, but February doesn't do too badly, either. Sprigs of pollen dangle from the tips of oak trees—spring's version of tinsel. Wind rushes through the treetops, shaking the branches clean. Swirls of yellow leaves rain down.

We walk into church and take our regular pew. I can't believe how normal we're acting! Mom sets up Libby on the space next to her, and Dad flips through the bulletin, both of them saying hello every now and then to people they know.

Though my lips are buttoned, the secret of You Know What beams out of my eyes anytime I look at someone. I radiate with You Know What. You Know What fills my stomach and leaks out of my pores. How can we just be *sitting*? We should be leaping with joy, shouting with happiness. Every good gift comes from God—that's what the Bible says—and if you can think of a better gift than *MILLIONS OF DOLLARS*, you'd better tell me because I can't.

Later, when the basket passes to me, I empty my peanut butter jar into it—my complete savings from the past year's allowance, birthday, Christmas, and lucky findings. Since buckets of money are coming my way, I feel good throwing some God's way.

The pastor's talking. I'm trying to listen. I reach forward, grab a bulletin from the holder, and nab one of those stubby pencils without erasers. Why does the church put out pencils without erasers? Makes me feel like I'm not allowed to make mistakes.

I turn the bulletin over to the place where you can take notes on the sermon.

11. Mansion

12. New backpack

13.

Mom swipes the notes and frowns. That's okay. Not to brag, but I have a good memory and by the time church lets out, I've added eight more things to my mental notes.

The pastor stands in the doorway and says good-bye to people. I'm surprised when he shakes my hand and twinkles his eyes at me. "Hailee, I couldn't help but notice you today."

My mouth drops open. God has told him! God has told him the secret! I am so relieved to finally be able to say something to someone. "Can you believe it? We're—"

"Hailee." Mom's using her TV-mother voice. "I think you interrupted the pastor."

"That's okay," he says. "I saw the joy of the Lord on your face today. I'd like to see that on more of our parishioners."

Not me, because I don't want to share that lottery money with anyone, except the Lord, of course. Still, I'm disappointed that the pastor didn't know why he saw the joy on my face because now I can't tell him.

When the van takes the usual left turn toward home, I stretch against my seat belt and pop my head between Dad and Mom in the front. "Let's go out to eat!" I say.

We can't go home to the same old boring grilled cheese and pickles we have every Sunday—we're millionaires.

Mom twists in her seat. "I've got to feed Libby and put her down for a nap."

Blah, blah, blah, boring.

"C'mon, Dad!" I say. "We need to celebrate!" When he dashes a hopeful glance at Mom, I know I've hooked him. "Eat, drink, and be merry!" I turn to Mom. "Ecclesiastes, eight fifteen." Brownie points for remembering a Bible verse.

Mom laughs. "Wow!" All her lines fade—the two lines that look like an eleven between her eyebrows, the lines that cup her mouth whether she smiles or frowns, and even the equator across her forehead—all gone. Her skin is cover girl dewy. She lays a hand on Dad's shoulder and raises her eyebrows.

"Say no more." Dad cranks the wheel and we U-turn toward downtown Orlando.

The car bumps over brick roads. I stare at the homes of Orlando's rich. Spanish moss hangs like lace from wide and twisted oak trees; some branches are so huge, they dip, touch the ground, and spring back up as big as another tree. We pass the brick two-story mansion I like, another one that sits on a pond, and then my favorite: the two-story yellow house with white columns and a brick circle drive. Pink and purple azaleas explode everywhere. Shiny cars crouched low like panthers line the driveway.

Just then, the front door opens. I get to see a real-life

rich person! It's a lady. Disappointing, because I wanted to pick up rich-kid tips, but still. She's tan and dressed in a skirty tennis outfit. Turning back to the house, she yells to someone inside as she gathers her dark hair into a ponytail.

No kids playing out front. Rich kids practice squash and polo; they don't play kickball in the street like common people.

I wonder which sport I will play.

We sit outside at a restaurant on Lake Eola. Torches are lit to keep everyone warm, and I'm glad because my goose pimples have their own goose pimples here in the shade.

A guy comes to our table wearing a white shirt, black pants, and a black vest. F–A–N–C–Y. "Hello, my name is William and I'll be taking care of you today."

Before William can say another word, I ask, "Do you have lobster?" I don't know if I like lobster, but I know it's expensive.

"Hailee!" Mom says.

William the Waiter chuckles. "Actually, we do have lobster bisque—"

Dad cuts him off. "Give us a minute, please." William bows out of the picture. I fold my arms and frown. At least Libby gets what she wants—Cheerios and juice—but the rest of us haven't ordered yet.

"Lobster?" Dad shakes open the kids' menu and sticks it in front of me.

"Dad." I push away the paper with mazes and tic-tac-toe on it. "I'm not a baby."

Mom peeks over her reading glasses. "Don't be difficult."

Libby throws Cheerios from her high chair. A pigeon struts across the patio on pink legs, pecking his shiny green head as he nears the rings of nutrition provided by my sister. The pecking must involve some kind of Morse code, because he's joined by other pigeons that crowd closer to the high chair.

"Aah!" Libby sprays them with another handful. A seagull dive-bombs from the sky and pushes his way to the front. I snatch some cereal and throw it to the pigeons in the back; they were here before Mr. Important I'm a Seagull.

Libby raises her little fist; in it is a lucky Cheerio—two circles stuck together. She squeals and waves the double Cheerio. The seagull unfolds his wings, opens them fully, then lifts off in a flurry of white and gray. I've never heard it so close: *whap, whap, whap!* I duck my head while Mom shoots up from her chair, flapping at the bird, but not before he's grazed Libby's hand and stolen the double ring. He touches down for a moment, then sails out over Lake Eola with Libby's lucky Cheerio. It's taken about three seconds for all this to happen.

Then the howling begins. She doesn't even warm up or anything, just lets out with the loudest, most horrifying, high-pitched wail ever emitted by a human. Mom tries to inspect Libby's hand, but Libby flails about in her high chair like a fish on dry land. I don't see any blood, so I'm guessing she was just scared. I steal Dad's menu and peruse my selections.

Other diners turn our way with their fake-sympathetic looks, which really mean, *Get that crying baby outta here! I'm trying to enjoy my shrimp!*

William the Waiter appears out of nowhere. "Anything I can do to help?"

Dad's standing up, trying to free Libby from the high chair as she bites his arms. "Ah—OW!"

"Ryan, help me . . ." Mom's hands wrap around Libby, lifting; Libby's hands wrap around Mom's hair, pulling.

William takes a step backward.

"We might need a minute," Dad says.

"I know what I want." I point to Dad's menu. "Lobster bisque!"

William raises his pencil, but instead of writing down my order, he chews on the eraser. "I'll give you folks a few more seconds."

"Dad!"

"Hailee!"

"Aa-ee! Aaee!" Libby's face is red. Gooey snot dribbles from her nose, and her fuzzy baby hair is damp with sweat.

Mom makes a hammock of her arms and swings

Libby. Mouths drop open. *Not child abuse*, I want to yell. *Saw it on TV.* But it doesn't work in real life—Libby outdoes herself; her squalling reaches octaves I've never heard before. Windows shatter; birds drop out of the sky; people's ears spurt blood. None of that happens, of course, but you get what I mean.

Grabbing the sippy cup and Mom's purse, Dad says, "You ready?" Mom's already halfway down the stairs from the restaurant.

"I'm hungry!" I say. "I want my lobster bisque!"

Dad swings Mom's purse onto his shoulder. "Come on."

"I could get it to go!" I call to his back. "Dad!"

He turns around, slumps his shoulders, and retraces his steps. "Hailee, your mom and I are tired. We stayed up all night long trying to figure out what we should do next. And this"—he gestures around the restaurant—"isn't working, so let's go."

My eyes water. This day started with sunshine, but Libby's ruined it with her storm clouds. I march behind Dad all the way to the car, where Mom is making Libby giggle in her car seat. By the time we get home, Libby is fast asleep. Anyone looking would coo at her. Mom slips her out of the car seat, and before I know it, everyone but me is taking a nap.

I pull out the frying pan and make a grilled cheese.

Chapter 5

. . . .

Money is the root of all evil.

What the Bible really says is that the *love* of money is the root of all evil, so that's how I know I'm not sinning; I don't love money—I just can't wait to lay my hands on it. The ticket sits in a secret hiding place in Mom and Dad's bedroom. They haven't claimed the money yet! They say they're thinking. Them thinking looks a lot like them staring out windows while their coffee gets cold on the table. They drift through the house like ghosts, Mom rattling her chain necklace and Dad moaning as he rises from chairs.

"Today? Can we get the money today?" I ask, dancing around them. I refill their coffee cups. I put carrot muffins on plates and push them across the table. I get Dad's good shoes and stick them in the front room, toes pointing forward so all he has to do is slide into them and go on out the door. *Not today*, one of them will say, and the shoes are carried back to the closet.

They are taking so long to get rich that the poor seeps into the framework of the house, causing it to groan against the March wind. Meanwhile, I'm supposed to not say anything about winning the lottery. Do you know how a secret grows inside of you every day you don't tell it? When I was little, I swallowed an apple seed and even though my mom said it wouldn't, I imagined that little seed growing into a big fat tree in my stomach. This secret is bigger than any apple tree. I feel it pressing against my ribs. I feel it straining for the light of day. For every word I speak, twenty more try to get out. You Know What is killing me.

"Vegetable," Mrs. Rice says. It's Thursday, the day of our weekly pretest. Mrs. Rice paces across the language arts classroom, dictating our vocabulary words. We not only have to spell them; we have to use them in sentences. "Vegetable."

My pencil goes to work:

> *If one hates the vegetable on the plate, especially if it is broccoli, one should simply ring the butler and order carrots.*

Satisfied, I wait for the next word.
"Equator."
I tap my pencil against my desk.

"Shh!" someone behind me snaps. I ignore her. Equator.

> *The equator divides the Earth into hemispheres,*
> *and we own mansions in both of them.*

I smile to myself. Good one.

"Last word, people," Mrs. Rice says. "Knowledge." She repeats it, but my sentence is already pouring onto the paper.

> *It's common knowledge that when a regular*
> *person talks to a millionaire, he or she should always*
> *bow or curtsy before them.*

I can't believe how every single spelling word has something to do with winning the lottery. It's almost as if Mrs. Rice knows. I stare at her as she collects our papers.

"Great spelling words," I say, watching her face for a revealing sign, like a wink or a smile that she tries to press down, but her face is the same Mrs. Rice face I see every second period.

The same thing happens in all my classes. In social studies, we talk about Henry Flagler, a rich guy in the old days; in math, we calculate the cost of a granite countertop; in science, we prepare to dissect clams, which sometimes have pearls.

By the time the bell rings, my hands are sweaty and

I'm nervous as a tick. I jump from my seat and rocket to the cafeteria. I spot Amanda at our table, rush over, and plop down across from her. The words that have been straining against the backs of my teeth finally pop out.

"If you won a million dollars, what would you buy with it?" Finally! I said it out loud. I feel like I do when the dentist puts that mask on my face. I want to giggle; I want to laugh; I want to leap onto the lunch table and shout.

Amanda considers the question between bites of the sub her mom made. I can see the layers: brown-sugared ham, oven-roasted turkey, Swiss cheese—all from Leonard's Deli downtown. Where *we'll* be able to shop now.

"Maybe a horse," she says.

"A horse?"

She shrugs.

As I open my lunchbox to my peanut butter and marshmallow sandwich, I think about a horse. Seems like something a rich girl should have.

"What else?" The peanut butter and marshmallow gum up my mouth, but Amanda understands me.

"A yacht."

"A yacht!" *All* rich people have yachts!

"An indoor pool. Home movie theater. Chandeliers."

My mental notes can hardly keep up with her.

Later that night, I add all her ideas to my list, which— even though I've crossed out a few things—still takes up two sides of a paper.

"Hailee!" Mom calls out gaily. The reason I said gaily is because it has the right old-fashioned ring to it and Mom is acting like the mother from *The Brady Bunch* or one of those other old TV shows where moms wear dresses and the house is always clean.

She's acting this way because tonight someone called a financial adviser is here to help Mom and Dad decide what to do with all our dough. I want to make sure the financial adviser knows all his options, so I hand copied the list of Things I Need and gave it to Dad. I was careful to not make any cross outs or erasing marks because you know how hard those can be to read.

The financial adviser talked to Mom and Dad all night long. I was supposed to watch Libby, and while my eyeballs stuck to her, my ear holes got extra sensitive, picking up secret information from the dining room. "College funds," "IRAs," and "installments." I didn't understand what they were talking about, and more important, *none* of that stuff is on my list.

The next day, Dad drove to Tallahassee for the money. I thought he'd race home with fat burlap bags of one hundred dollar bills sitting belted neatly into their seats, but he came home empty-handed. "They're wiring the money over," he told us when Mom, Libby, and I rushed him at the door. Mom said she was glad he was safe. I was glad the money was safe; I got worried when I didn't see those bags.

Nothing about winning the lottery was turning

out the way I thought it would. I wanted to go out to eat; they wanted to take a nap. I wanted to go to the movies; they said just watch TV. I wanted to have a party and they said we need to be alone right now.

Mom shuffled around telling Dad we must be good stewards. The pastor uses that word a lot in church; a steward is a person who takes care of something, especially stuff that has been given to you—like money. *Good stewards*, Mom would mumble. *Good stewards*, Dad droned in return.

Not even when the Action 5 Reporter Live stopped by did they get excited. The reporter practically jumped out of his pants when Dad started telling how it all happened. Of course, Libby being a baby, she just babbled, but still the Action Reporter thought it was cute and he had the camera man zoom in on her, and that's when I dropped my photo pose because usually when people get all caught up with Libby, my part of the show's over. Then he stuck the microphone in my face. The camera pointed at me. A red light shone on the top. I forgot which side of my face I had practiced in the mirror.

"Would you repeat the question?" I asked the Action 5 Reporter Live.

His rows of white teeth flashed. He had makeup on. And hair spray. I noticed all this in the time it took him to say, "How do you plan to spend your winnings?"

I froze.

"Look into the camera," he whispered through his unnaturally white smile. If he ever lost his job as a reporter, he could be a ventriloquist.

I looked straight into that camera and forgot everything I wanted to tell it. The Action Reporter hissed. Dad cleared his throat. Only Mom cast a life-saving glance at me, and then I remembered something to say.

"I want to be a good stewardess."

The Action 5 Reporter Live laughed heartily and told Michelle at the station, "Back to you."

Suddenly they were wrapping up their cords, folding down their lights, walking out of our house.

"Oh, my gosh." I ran down the steps as the Action Reporter climbed into the passenger side of the van. "That's not what I meant to say!"

He slammed the door shut and flashed me his teeth. "Good spot. You were great!"

"No! I don't want to be a stewardess!"

"You'll figure it out!" The van pulled away from our driveway and straight to my embarrassment.

★   ★   ★

"Hey, you're that millionaire girl!" a boy shouts as I pass him on my way to school Monday morning.

I almost fall off my ugly red bike. "Thank you!" I yell over my shoulder, realizing as I say it that it isn't quite the right response.

Up ahead, a group of girls clogs the sidewalk. They

shuffle along, lollygagging as one of them stops to rummage inside her backpack. Slowpokes. My first car will have a radar detector so I can speed around Sunday drivers without getting a ticket.

The grass is mushy and hard to pedal through, but it's the only way to get past the slower-than-snails girls.

"Wait a second!" yells one with a streak of blue hair.

Uh-oh. Hope I didn't splash her with mud or something. I slow down.

Blue Hair Streak whirls around to her friends. "It *is* her! I told you!" She turns starry eyes toward me. "I saw you on TV last night! You're the girl who won the lottery, right?"

"Um, yeah." I stop the bike and put my foot down, but I can't think of anything else to say. It doesn't seem to matter. The four of them get big cow eyes and stare at me as if I were a celebrity.

They move closer, slowly, without seeming to realize it.

"Three million dollars," one of them says.

"What?" another shrieks.

"If *I* won three million dollars," says Blue Hair Streak, "you wouldn't catch me coming to school!"

Ooh, good point. I tuck that thought away as a possibility for my list of Things I Need.

"Well," I say, "I gotta get going."

Blue Hair Streak nudges one of the other girls. "Move, Trish. You're in her way."

All four of them scoot into the grass while I pedal onto the sidewalk.

"Bye!" they call out. "Don't spend it all in one place!"

I crook my head around, giving them a perfect over-the-shoulder pose. I add a tiny smile to let them know I appreciate their humor.

The sidewalk down the school entrance becomes a red carpet, with people clamoring after me and shouting questions. "Hailee, over here!" "Hey, *I* was going to talk to her!" Kids I hardly know ask if I need help locking up my bike or carrying my backpack. Their faces gleam in my presence. Their feet work to keep up with me.

I had no idea all this was going to happen, yet I've been preparing for it my whole life.

"Hailee! Hailee!" Amanda runs up to me from the bicycle pen, her cheeks flushed, her arms wide open. Everyone makes room for her because she's my costar. She almost knocks me off my bike with a great big hug. "Oh, my gosh! Someone told Becca you won the lottery, but I told her *no way* because you would've called me—"

"I—"

"Then people started asking me if it was true—"

"It—"

"So I called your mom!" Amanda's eyes gleam like they do when she drinks too much Mountain Dew. "YOU GUYS ARE RICH!"

"I KNOW!" Our capital letter words skip across the waves of love and attention surging toward us—well, really *me*, because I am The Girl Who Won The Lottery.

When the bell calls us to class, everyone stops what they're doing as I walk by; I hear them start up again only after I've passed. Teachers and students alike strain for a glimpse or a word from me.

Cottony puffs of feel-good vibes stuff my brain. I hear and see everything around me, but it's like I'm floating in a bubble. My feet don't feel the floor. Think of this: your best birthday when you finally for once get everything you really want. The cake isn't lopsided, and after your friends and parents sing "Happy Birthday," someone adds, *and many more*, then everyone laughs. *That's* how good being famous feels.

When Becca slides her hot lunch tray onto the table, she hunches her shoulders. "Here they come," she says.

Amanda's eyes flit up, then she studies her milk carton as if there'll be a test on chocolate milk later.

"I want to be a stewardess," Megan mimics as I unwrap my peanut butter sandwich. Oh, no—she obviously saw me on the news last night. She and Drew stop at the table Amanda, Becca, and I sit at.

"Peanuts? Pretzels?" Megan pretends to ask airline passengers as she paces behind me. "They're not called stewardesses anymore; they're *flight attendants*."

"Yeah," Drew sneers at me.

I look across the table at Amanda, but she puts her head down. Searching for just the right comeback, my mind stumbles through huge blank spaces. At this point in the situation, Megan usually fires her kill shot, but here's where winning the lottery comes in handy—my new fans come to the rescue, pushing Megan and Drew away, literally squeezing past them to join me on the bench.

"What's it like being rich?" "Are you moving to a mansion?" "Are you buying a jet?" I laugh at the thought of piloting an airplane to school. For one thing, where would I land it?

"Not a jet," I say, thinking. "But probably a limo."

One boy asks why Mom is still delivering the newspaper. When Dad asked her the same thing last week, she said, *I just . . . wanted to wait until I knew it was real.*

It's real, Dad had said and cracked a lopsided smile. *You'd better believe it.*

Now curious faces want to know why a millionaire gets up at four in the morning to hurl newspapers into their driveways. I say, "She wanted to give her two weeks' notice."

The boy snorts. "I would've quit!"

I frown.

Another girl says her dog had diarrhea on the good rug, and her mom is going to call my dad to come take care of the stain. Everyone groans and a couple of the boys make retching sounds. I feel each of the seven layers of my skin turn red.

Amanda goes, "She can't help it if her dad cleans carpet."

"Amanda!" Oh, my gosh—she's making it worse.

I wriggle from the bench like a worm. I am pink and gross, with everybody stepping on me. The worst part, the part I can't take, is that they are right. Mom should have quit her stupid newspaper job. Dad cleaning dog poop? What's wrong with my parents? We're *rich* now—other people should be doing this stuff for *us*.

Amanda follows me to my locker. Some kids try to stop me in the hall, but I don't talk. Talking will just make this feeling grow bigger. Later, when the dismissal bell rings, I'm the first one out the door, the first one in the pen, and the only one riding a three-dollar bike.

I yank my stupid bike off the kickstand and rasp away. Red bike and green shirt—look at me, I'm the biggest dork in the universe. I pound the pedals all the way home. I'm going so fast that when I hit our driveway, the wheels roll right through the brakes as I try to stop, the seat bucks me off, and I scurry away before it falls on top of me. Dusting off my shorts, I kick the bike. It makes a screechy sound as it slides across the garage floor. "Stupid bike!"

I grab it by the horns, wrestle it up, and knock it into its resting place. "I'm getting a new one," I tell it.

A lizard skitters through a hole between the cinder blocks. "New garage!" I yell.

As I walk out, a bougainvillea branch sticks me with a pricker. "New plants!" I yell at the vine, which sways in the wind as if readying for another attack.

★   ★   ★

Oak trees shimmer with tender leaves the second week of March. The parched grass sucks up the spring rain and colors each blade with green. Orange blossoms decorate their trees like ornaments, filling the air with a scent so pretty, you could actually believe in fairies. Even the lovebugs are starting up.

Everything in nature has been renewed.

Nothing in the Richardson house has been renewed. My cheery red maple is not so cheery anymore, dropping its leaves as if it no longer has the energy for them. A shock of red puddles around the tree, but as days go by, time drains the color and makes the leaves crispy and brown.

One night at supper, I ask Dad why he bothers going to work.

"We still need an income," he says, grabbing the mashed potatoes.

"We won the lottery," I say in a *Dad-did-you-forget* voice.

"Yes, but we're not rich." Dad keeps a straight face as he says this.

I try to stare him down, but I lose and start laughing first. "Yeah, right! Good one."

"Hailee," Mom says. "Remember we told you how it works? We're taking the money as installments—that means we get a little money each year, enough that I can quit the newspaper and not take on any Christmas jobs."

What?

Mom's mouth keeps moving, but all I hear is this: *Blah blah blah* college fund. *Blah blah* investments *blah* future *blahaha mwahaha mwahahaha! Mwahahaha!*

I snap out of it. "College? That's years away! What about the stuff we could use right now? I thought winning the lottery would change our lives, but I still don't have a good bike or new clothes or anything! Where's my cell phone? Where's my computer? I need a new backpack." My words flash like a sharp sword. I home in on Mom before delivering the final blow. "You don't even know what it takes to get good grades."

The hurt in her eyes tells me I've struck a vital chord.

"That's enough," Dad says in a husky voice. "Don't ever disrespect your mother like that." He covers her hand with his.

I lower my head. I guess I did cross the line there. "Sorry," I say.

Dad clears his throat. "Your mother and I have been talking—more than talking. We're enrolling you in the Magnolia Academy for Girls."

"What?" My voice scrapes the ceiling.

Silence.

"I said I was sorry!"

Dad shakes his head. "It doesn't have anything to do with that. The curriculum there is supposed to be excellent. Magnolia was listed in the paper as one of the top private schools in the area. Mom visited last Friday and she was very impressed."

"No! I said I was sorry!" Desperate, my eyes seek forgiveness from my mom. "I don't need a phone or a computer or any of that stuff. You don't have to buy me anything." I'll eat bread and butter the rest of my days. I'll use newspapers as blankets. "Just please don't make me switch schools."

"Hailee," Mom says, stretching her hand out to me. I don't take it. "We were lucky—their principal said the quarter just ended and it's the perfect time to start." Her voice becomes reverent. "This is the opportunity of a lifetime."

Stumbling up from my chair, I wipe the tears away. "It's the *punishment* of a lifetime! You hate me."

Mom's mouth drops.

Dad starts to say something, but I wave away his words. "You both hate me!" I yell, and before they can say anything else, I run upstairs, slam the door, and lock it.

Imprisoned in my own room. Without even the phone so I can call Amanda.

I am truly alone.

Chapter seventeen is where I'm at in *Because of Winn-Dixie*. Opal has met a girl named Amanda and they don't like each other but you can tell they're going to be friends. Since I read a lot of books, I know stuff like that. Anyway, there is nothing but sadness in this chapter. Opal eats a piece of candy and it reminds her how lonely she is, and the first thing she says about loneliness is how she misses all her friends from where she used to live. I know exactly how she feels. Moving to a new school will be just like moving to a new town—I won't know anyone and no one will know me.

I am just like Opal. I even have a friend named Amanda *and* I live in Florida. If they make a sequel to the movie, I should probably play Opal's part. I wonder if I should write to the author and tell her.

The next chapter is even sadder. If you want to know why, I can't tell you. You have to read it for yourself, but don't skip right to that part just because you want to know what I'm talking about.

I close the book and let it rest on my stomach. Then tears leak from my eyes, sliding into my hair and making wet spots on my bedspread. We *won* the lottery. Winning isn't supposed to make you lose things.

Chapter 6

. . . .

I cried all night and Amanda had tears this morning when I spilled the news.

"But why?" she asked between blubbery sobs. "We're an A school!"

That's true—I saw it on the school sign by the road.

Amanda folded into her chair. The bell hadn't rung yet, so I sank into the desk behind her. "But we have homeroom and lunch together. We're going to be in Compass Club next year."

Her watery eyes look into mine.

Lisa, the girl whose desk I'm sitting at, sees our tears. She lowers her backpack. "What's wrong?"

"She's moving to a different school." Amanda's voice cracks.

Lisa bends down to Amanda with a look of pure

sympathy. "That's terrible." Everyone knows we are best friends. Then she asks me, "Where're you going?"

I pour as much glum as I can into my answer. I want her to pat my shoulder and make me feel better, too. "Magnolia."

"Magnolia!" Instead of consoling me, she congratulates me. She wants to know all about it. Then the bell rings and I go off to my own seat.

The whole day I notice things I've taken for granted: the plastic red-shouldered hawk that looks out of the library window; the way the cafeteria lady says, "Enjoy your lunch"; the loud, happy voices in the hallway between classes. Magnolia won't be like this. It's a private school—that's practically like going to a military academy.

After school, when Amanda and I part ways on our bikes, she hugs me as if I'm moving overseas.

That does it. They haven't signed me away yet. I'm not going to Magnolia. I will inform Mom as soon as I get home. I ride my red boy bike home, slam it into the garage, and march into the house.

"*¿Cómo te llamas? Buenos días. Buenos días. Buenosbuenosbuenos días.*"

What the heck? The tangy scent of lemon bread greets me at the door. The smell is so powerful, especially when you know how the sugary lemony glaze tingles on your tongue, and your face can't decide if it wants to screw up for the tartness or relax for the sweetness. The only way to decide is to take another bite. My mouth is already watering, but first, I must detect who the Spanish-speaking lady is.

I slide my backpack to the floor, creep near the kitchen, and peek around the doorway to see who's over. Using expert spy maneuvers, I angle my head and use my left eye as a periscope. Mom's pouring hot lemon syrup from the frying pan over two yellow loaves of lemon bread. This is one of the rare cases in which you definitely want the heel because that's where all the syrup ends up. Looking past her to the table, I see no one.

"Hola."

With precision swiftness, my laser eyes fall upon Libby. She's examining a red, blue, yellow, and white toy with all kinds of whizbangs and buttons. It looks like fun.

"Hi, Mom," I say, coming out from my hiding place. My eyes slide over that lemon bread.

"Nope!" She knows my plan. "Wait till it cools."

"Hola," the toy says.

"Aa-ee! Aa-ee!" Libby's smile makes her chubby cheeks even chubbier. She toddles toward me, waving her arms in excitement. Little pink shorts bloom over her diaper.

"Libby!" I scoop her up and kiss her tummy. "Libby! Libby-Libby-Lou!" It tickles so much, she can hardly stand it. She shrieks with laughter and struggles at the same time.

I set her down by the toy and mash a button. *"Me*

llamo say your name." The lady sounds very patient. I press the button again and wait for the cue. "*Me llamo.*" "Hailee," I fill in, then I push the playback button.

"*Me llamo* Hailee."

I like it.

Libby pesters me over the next few minutes as I record and play back the names of our family and neighbors. She keeps reaching her stubby fists over and, finally, she mashes the record button, erasing my voice.

"Stop it!" Using my arm as a guard, I keep her away while I list my classmates.

But arm guard or not, the levers and purple smiley face with workable features aren't enough for her; she's got to do what I'm doing. She pulls and tugs at my shirt, not even looking at the toy now—she's all about getting me.

"Stop it!" I snarl. It's just a gentle push I give her, hardly a push at all—more like a tap, or a touch—but it's enough to make her fall onto her puffy behind and wail. Happily, I search my mental databanks for another name to record.

"Hailee, why is she crying? Can you change her diaper?"

"*Me llamo.*" "Diaper." Ha! I crack myself up.

Libby leans over and sinks her sharp little teeth into my arm.

"YEOW!" I jerk my arm away, a move that knocks

her on her butt, complete with full-scale wailing and tears.

Mom gives me the eyebrow.

"She bit me!"

The eyebrow, amazingly, arches higher. Mom tamps the syrup-covered spoon against the loaf pans and holds it up. Why, yes—I *would* like to lick it. I'm up and across the room in a flash, but Mom's faster. She holds the spoon just out of my reach.

"Go tell her you're sorry."

"She won't even know what I'm saying."

The spoon moves farther away.

My shoulders droop, and I trudge over to Libby to make amends. She's busy hitting buttons. I pat her back, say I'm sorry, and that's when I notice the crisp, white price tag on the side of the toy.

"Did you buy this at the store?"

Mom smiles. "Isn't it neat? I just went for some teething stuff and . . ." She shrugs her shoulders.

"It's okay."

"Oh"—she points with the spoon—"and I got that stuffed rocking horse in the corner. Libby loves it!"

I charge up the stairs. My new stuff is probably on my bed, where Libby can't swipe it or put it in her mouth. But my bed is just as I left it. My closet hasn't been touched. I pull open my drawers, slam them shut, then clobber down the stairs so fast I nearly crash into the island. "What did you get for me?" I say between breaths.

The syrup-laden spoon sits in a lemony puddle on a saucer. My question doesn't stop Mom from rinsing the baking dishes. "What?" she asks over the noise of the faucet.

I raise my voice. "Where's my stuff? What did you buy for me?"

Mom turns off the water, shakes the silverware, and puts it into the dishwasher. "I was at the baby store, honey; they don't have things for girls your age." She says it like I should know that.

"But you could've gone somewhere else." Easy enough to swing by and get something for your other daughter, who was thoughtful enough to make up a list of things she needs.

Mom goes to stroke my hair, but I duck from her hand. She says, "Don't be mad. I ran errands all day today, and my last stop was the baby store. I was so tired by then, I put Libby in their play area and sat in one of those gliders for a while watching her. She had so much fun."

Well. What a good day for Libby.

"One of my errands was dropping off the forms to Magnolia."

"I don't want to go there."

Mom doesn't say anything. Instead, she tries to reel

me in with the oldest trick in the book. "Are you going to lick that spoon or am I going to wash it?"

Silently, I raise the spoon to my mouth, but then I see a smile of satisfaction flicker across my mom's face. Licking this spoon means I have to go to Magnolia. Though I would love to slurp off every last lemony drop and wash the spoon clean with my tongue, I steel myself against its power. It takes all my strength to set the spoon down.

"What's wrong?" Mom asks.

I throw out my words without caring where they land. "Too bitter," I say. And before I shoot out the door, I add, "I'm not going to Magnolia."

Then I'm gone.

Chapter 7

. . . .

Rrish, rrish, riiish.

I pedal down Crape Myrtle Road.

Rrish, rrish, riiish.

Orange blossoms spangle in the trees. I slow way down; in fact, I stop. I walk my bike through the gravel edge of the road and up to the barbed-wire fence that holds in the orange trees. The creamy blossoms breathe softly, wisps of their light orangey fragrance washing the air. If factories could make air fresheners that really smelled like this, nobody would ever be mad or fight or do anything bad—that's how pretty orange blossoms smell.

Bees murmur through the trees, landing for seconds on the blossoms, then flying off to the next. They sound like gangs of tiny motorcycles. A big black-and-reddish-orange butterfly darts over, and just as the word "monarch" forms in my mind, I realize this "butterfly" has a long needle beak, feathers, and sash of neon red around her neck. Against the green leaves and white flowers, the little bird stands out beautifully. I watch, just staring, thankful for this moment. Some people go their whole lives without once seeing a hummingbird in real wildlife. Counting this one, I have now seen two. I click its picture by blinking and file it in my mental notes.

"Ruby-throated hummingbird."

I shriek and almost impale myself on the fence. "Emily DeCamp," I say, snatching my bike up from the scrabbly grass.

She stands there like I shouldn't be surprised to see her. Her blue Magnolia skirt comes to just above her knees, and tucked into it is her stiff, white button-down top. Her arms hang at her sides, one hand holding her notebook. Springy hair bounces down her neck, under and over her collar, and even covers part of her face. Bees could get lost in it.

"You're coming to Magnolia." She says this like it's a fact, but her voice comes out rushed. The eye that I can see through the hair beams with hope.

"No, I'm not. I go to Palm Middle." I grab both my bike handles and roll slowly out to the road. Emily DeCamp follows me.

"I saw your mother in the office last week." She consults her notebook.

I glance over. Emily DeCamp's handwriting is a

perfect rhythm of cursive loops and dips that flow from side to side in unwavering margins. I am impressed. "Let me see that."

She clutches it close.

The March breeze envelops us both in the perfume of the orange blossoms, and Emily DeCamp and I take in a deep breath at the same time. We walk on the correct side of the road, which is the side facing the cars, *so you can see them when they hit you*, as my dad likes to say. My bike rasps as we go, but Emily doesn't mention it. I hadn't planned where I was going, but this is where I seem to have ended up.

"Your mother was at my school today again."

I shrug my shoulders.

Emily DeCamp sneaks another look at her notebook.

Why does she always have that thing? "Why do you always have that thing?"

"I'm going to be a writer." She sticks a finger through her hair and pushes her glasses up. "I'm on the yearbook staff."

We stop directly across from her house.

"I have to practice my flute now," she says. "Are you getting a new bike?"

So she did notice the rusty hacking of my old boy bike.

"Since you won the lottery, you could get a new bike like Amanda's."

Is she a mind reader? That's the first thing on my list. "How did you know?"

A sliver of eyeball considers me through the hair. "I am observant," she says. "But don't worry, you won't need to ride your bike to Magnolia." Her head swivels left, then right, then left again.

"I'm not going to Magnolia," I yell to her back as she crosses the street. She hops up the curb and over the stepping stones to her porch. "I go to Palm Middle!" Up the porch steps, through the screen door. "Scratch that part out of your notebook—my mom was just visiting. I'm not going to school there."

Weeds wind around my ankle, prickling my skin. I trample them. Emily DeCamp is wrong. I'm not going to her school. I get on my bike and pedal home.

Rrish! Rish! I rish people would listen to me.

Chapter 8

· · · · · · · · · · · · · · · · ·

The stone, impenetrable towers of Magnolia Academy for Girls stab the downtown sky; I can see them through the trees as Mom drives over the brick roads. My teeth rattle in my head, but I don't think the bricks are doing it. "Is this good on the van?" I ask as if it's the van I'm thinking about.

"Don't worry, honey, this van is a tank." She gives me a reassuring smile as if I actually *want* to get to Magnolia. "Green light," she says. We move with the other cars like a string of beads being pulled forward.

When you're eager to get somewhere, say someone's birthday party or an ice cream place, it takes forever. When you don't want to get somewhere, green lights smile their permission to fly through intersections. There are no trucks to get stuck behind, no squirrels to hit the brakes for, and even Libby falls into a cozy sleep.

I pull a finger around the stiff collar of my white top, part of my uniform for Magnolia Academy for Girls, which we got at JC Penney, along with the blue skirt and blue shorts. *Kind of expensive, aren't they?* I asked when I showed Mom the price tags at the store. *The principal said three of each*, I reminded her as we searched for my size through the clothing racks, *three times each price tag.* I squished my round feet into pointy black shoes. *These hurt*, I said. *My feet don't end in a point.*

Quit whining, Mom said.

As the van passes my favorite house, the yellow one with white pillars, a woman dressed like she could never be someone's mom steps out from the front door; it's the tennis lady, with a girl right behind her. Blue skirt, white blouse. My heart flips a beat. Could this girl be going to my school? I sink down in my seat so she can't see me, but I can see her. Tan legs move like a gazelle's as she prances down the steps. She's not wearing knee socks like I have to—she must be an eighth grader. They're required to wear stockings. Her mom, if she is her mom, says something to the girl, but the girl doesn't like it because she rolls her eyes, jerks her head, and saunters back into the house.

She doesn't want to go, either!

I bet the teachers are mean and hit kids with rulers. Bars slam down over the classroom windows when the bell rings—no one can escape—and when the teacher asks a question, the girls answer in one voice like androids. At lunch, they file in robotically and sit on hard benches, staring forward while the headmistress watches, her boots clomping ominously as she paces in front of them. Mom didn't mention any of this, but that's because they probably put on a big act when visitors are there.

The woman who doesn't look like a mom gets out of her shiny car and crosses her arms. If I were an owl, I would turn my head backward and keep watching, but Mom has cleared the stop sign and we're creeping forward. Suddenly, I ram my door open, tear around the corner, and run full speed ahead to Palm Middle, my butt hitting the seat just as the tardy bell rings. That's what I wish I could do anyway, and maybe I would if I had my sneakers on because I'm faster than light with those on my feet. But what I've got on now—these black flats—pinch my toes and have slippery soles.

"This sure is a long drive," I say.

"I don't mind," Mom says. "I kind of miss my morning drives."

Does she have to be so cheerful about it? It's easy for her—she's not the one facing a world of strangers. Not only did she wear her best dress when she went on the tour, she also wore makeup. Blackened eyelashes, creamy foundation, pink pearly lips—she'd done more for Magnolia than she does for God every Sunday. I even smelled her perfume.

The Lake Eola fountain shimmers in the morning

sunlight. Little kids swirl down the curly slides of the playground. I wish I could join them. Tall buildings flank us as we come up to the corner. People in business clothes walk quickly on the sidewalks, wearing earpieces and talking into the air. Mom turns, and then the downtown Orange County Public Library is on our left. The best library ever. It's probably as big as the Library of Congress and has just as many books. Plus, it has elevators, a snack bar, and a basement, which is rare in Florida.

Mom frowns at the library. "I don't remember passing that before."

"Are we lost?" Because if we are, just park so I can run past the scary people who hang outside the library and dash to the children's section for the latest Margaret Peterson Haddix book.

"No, we're not lost. I have to figure out the side streets." She pulls up to a metered space and unfolds a map. By the way she squints at it, I can tell the words are playing musical chairs with her eyes. Leaning over, I spot the street we're on and the address she's got circled.

"Just go straight," I say, "then go right, right, left."

"Right, right, left."

"Right," I answer.

"I thought you said left."

"No, I—"

She breaks into a smile. "Just kidding. Right, right, left."

"Har, har," I say. Normally, I would think of something funny to say back, but my stomach's upset and my fingers feel twitchy.

We're heading into the heart of downtown. We pass houses with wraparound porches and second-story balconies. Antique tea roses sit in groups, pale pink and cream, like old ladies at church. They bow their heads as a light breeze snuffles over them.

As Mom makes the turns, I see the wrought-iron fence that surrounds the grounds of Magnolia. My heart starts beating for real. Only a few short minutes separate me from my fate.

A huge magnolia tree anchors one corner of the lawn. Under it, a girl about my age sits prettily with a set of paints and a sketchbook. The breeze flutters her paper, then tickles the top of the grass, leaving the velvety green tips to settle in an entirely different direction than before.

Mom glances through my window. "She might be one of your classmates."

True. I consider the girl, so entranced in her work that she takes no notice of our van as we pass. Two more girls come out from the side door of a nearby building, and the three of them twitter like birds, their wings fluttering as they arrange themselves in a circle on the grass. They don't look like they're in school; they look like they're having a picnic. I almost think, *They're so lucky*, before I remember I hate Magnolia.

"Should they be out here by themselves, Mom? It doesn't seem safe," I comment innocently.

"They're okay—they're fenced in. Besides, the building's right there."

We're here. Drums beat in my chest and echo in my arms and head. Heat flashes in my face. Sweat pops out of my skin even though the rest of me feels cold. Mom pulls up to the main entrance gate. All my brain cells scream, *NO! NO! NO!*

The Bible says there's a season and a time for everything, including a time to weep and mourn. Casting my eyes upon Magnolia Academy, my heart decides it's time to weep and mourn. My cheery red maple has lost its leaves. It will grow new ones, but they'll be plain and green and look like every other tree. When I glance through my bedroom window, I'll see something ordinary, and soon it will be hard to remember the exact watermelon hue of the leaves. No matter what happens today, I will never forget Palm Hill Middle School.

The man at Magnolia's security gate can't find our name. Maybe God has intervened, erased us from this list, and Mom will have to drive me straight to my real middle school.

Tears bubble up for the end of the maple. Why does it have to change? Why? Why? Why? I liked it the way it was—happy and energetic—the shock of those red leaves against the starkness of the white trunk. If it has to wear green leaves, it'll lose its mapleness. Tears spew from my eyes. Why can't things ever stay the same?

Mom hands over her ID. The security guard inspects it, studies Mom's face, then talks into a headpiece.

My eyes are thunderclouds swollen with tears. My mouth sucks in the last few breaths of freedom. My throat lumps up as I choke down my destiny.

"Hailee?"

I try to say "What?" but it comes out all gurgled, more like, "Wharg?"

"Hailee!" Mom brushes my hair off my forehead and that's all it takes. Tears wash down my face, drip off the edges, and soak into my white Magnolia Academy for Girls blouse.

"Ma'am?" The security guy hands Mom a clipboard.

Taking it, she says to me, "I'm sorry, honey," and then she works on a form while I silently cry.

I pull down the visor and check myself in the mirror.

Yes, I am miserable. Look how red my eyes are, my cheeks. Everything is wet or running, and strands of hair stick to the sides of my face. I watch myself sob, which makes me cry even harder because I see how forlorn I am.

I wonder how the Magnolia girls will see me.

I stop all the weeping, wipe my face, and stare at my reflection. My mouth pulls into a frown, but I force those muscles to relax because frowning's the ugliest part of crying. My eyebrows squinch, giving off just the right degree of despair. Tears sparkle in my eyes and glide down my face in crystal drops. I could be a girl in a movie who was taken by robbers but escaped and now must find her way back home through a huge black city with skyscrapers and dark alleys. I look at *this* girl in the mirror. She doesn't let tears stop her from getting home. She is noble and strong. I watch as another tear slides down her cheek. *This* is how I will cry from now on.

"Here we go," Mom says after collecting her ID from the guard. She fishes a used tissue from her purse, but the new me waves it away. Bravely, I fix my face forward, watching Magnolia appear before me as Mom pulls the van up the drive and parks in a visitor's spot.

I'm no longer in my body as it steps out of the van and hoists the official school backpack onto burdened shoulders. Another magnolia tree stands in front of the office building. The sweet scent of a goblet-sized blossom rides on a gentle breeze that encircles me, but I breathe out of my mouth to show that tree I'm not having any of it.

The office is in a small, yellow, steepled building. There's no cross on it, but it used to be a church when Orlando was nothing but orange groves; that's what it says in the brochure Mom brought home. She tugs the handle on one of the arched, honey-colored wooden doors, but it doesn't budge. "Oh, that's right," she says and presses an intercom button on the side. She squishes me in a side hug.

A disembodied voice asks if it can help us.

"I'm Kristen Richardson?" she tells it. "My daughter is starting school today?"

I wish she wouldn't talk in question marks—it makes her sound nervous. The voice tells her how wonderful it is that we're here and to open the door when we hear the buzzer.

I would like to tell you that the buzzer sounds like a chain saw going through green wood or the dentist's drill breaking your teeth, but I can't. The buzzer sounds like an electric organ holding a note.

Mom heaves the old door open with a big *whoosh* as the inside air gets sucked into the outside air and for a moment I think we could still change our minds because our feet have not yet crossed the threshold.

Mom presses her hand against the small of my back and pushes me toward my future.

Chapter 9

· · · · · · · · · · · · · · · ·

The first time I ever went inside Palm Middle was on a field trip in fifth grade. They loaded us up in buses and drove us across the back roads, and we got to see what it was going to be like to be middle schoolers. The tour started outside the office area, where a red-shouldered hawk stares out from a mural. The teachers gathered us in front of it and gave a speech about the red-shouldered hawk being Palm Middle's mascot and about school spirit and pride. When we walked away, I felt the hawk's eyes following me wherever I went.

I don't know what Magnolia's mascot is, probably a magnolia. The red-shouldered hawk would rip off its leaves, tear its bark, and strip the branches, carrying the scraps somewhere high and safe to make a nest. *Kee-aah! Kee-aah! Take that!* it would screech.

"Everything you need is in this folder: schedule, map, and student ID," the lady behind the counter says. She has a wrinkle for every year she's been here—I figure about a hundred.

"Well," Mom says. If she could go with me to every class, I know she would.

"Well," I say back. I love her, but the longer she stays, the more anxious I'll get. I kiss her on the cheek to make her feel better and then watch her shadow follow her out, slipping through those double doors right before they close on its neck.

My first class is math, which is room 221. I hoist my backpack up, a ridiculous effort because in it is only one binder with loose-leaf paper and dividers, a composition book, and a brown lunch bag, which, if I'm correct and I know I am, has a peanut butter and marshmallow sandwich, a banana, a juice box, and a note from Mom that probably says *I love you!* or *You can do it!*

Wrinkles stares at me from the counter. "Do you need some help with the map?"

I come from Palm Middle. I am a red-shouldered hawk. "I can find my way."

Wrinkles smiles at me. "Good luck. You're going to love it here."

I have to admit I do kind of like this building. The pine floor is poured like syrup on a waffle, and its sweet, knotty smell brings a peace to my heart. As I walk over it, I see the scuffs and dents left by a history of girls, maybe even Wrinkles herself. I wonder what mark I will leave here. If I even stay here, I mean.

Once I'm outside, the buildings look the same as one another, but definitely not like a regular school. The two-story buildings are stuccoed with pale gold and accented with white. Cobblestone paths cut through lawns so green, if you tried to draw it, you'd have to press hard with your green crayon to make sure you didn't leave any white spaces. Girls stroll in pairs or hang in groups under the trees.

The red-shouldered hawk is solitary.

I'm about to unfold my map when I see a number 1 on the building to my left. The building behind it must be number 2, so I start down the path while tucking the map into the side of my backpack. *Bam*! The red-shouldered hawk smashes into a Magnolia and causes her to stumble.

Everything happens fast, but my hawk eyes take it all in like a computer scan. Magnolia girl: golden brown hair; tall; no knee socks; and her blouse is filled out in a way that embarrasses me for noticing. "I'm sorry! I'm sorry! I didn't mean to knock you down." Oh, great— way to go, Hailee. My legs lock as I wait for her to turn around.

When she does, her face is furi-*endly*. I thought she would be furious, which is why I started to say furious, but she smiles and pretends to wipe her brow. "Whew! No runs." She's talking about her stockings. "You know how Mrs. Novey is about that!" Then she lopes off, joins some other girls in the grass, and they raise a chant about Magnolia.

Cheerleaders! That nice girl is a cheerleader. It makes perfect sense and none at all. Tall and pretty—*of course* she's a cheerleader; but then add nice and friendly. *Nice, friendly cheerleader.* See what I mean? This is what's known as an oxymoron, like jumbo shrimp—words that are put together but are opposites. Jumbo shrimp. Nice cheerleader. Think about it.

Knock, knock.

Who's there?

Ox.

Ox who?

Ox, you moron.

You can use that joke if you want to. I just made it up.

The bell rings and all across the grounds girls lift up their backpacks, straighten their white shirts, and flock to the cobblestones. I go with the flow, easing around building 1 to building 2, only it's not 2, it's 4. A little square building sits in the shadow—that *must* be 2—but as I hurry across the path, slinking through obstacles as if I'm at a skating rink, I discover this is building 3.

I spin around. I see 1, 4, and 3. Where's 2? I swing my backpack off for the map, but it's not there. It must have fallen out when I bumped into that girl. Blinking wide, I take in quick breaths heavy with the scent of magnolia trees.

"Do you know where building two is?" I ask a girl rushing by.

She points without stopping. "That way, past four."

Past 4 is 5, and past 5 is 6. The tardy bell rings and I am alone in the yard, about to cry.

Chapter 10

. . . .

GIRLS.

Of course the restroom is for girls. It's a girls-only school.

Pushing the door open, I let my tears fall because the last thing I'm expecting to see is a girl leaning against the tiled walls smoking. And not just any girl, either—she's the girl from the yellow house, the girl who didn't want to come to school today, the girl who pranced back into her house with her tan legs.

She's even prettier up close. Her dark hair is short, but cut in long layers with bangs that nearly hide her huge blue eyes. She raises the cigarette to her lips, and the fiery end lights up as she inhales.

"This bathroom's reserved." Her words are smoke. She flicks ashes into a sink.

Stupid, stupid, stupid me. "I'm sorry." My voice quavers. "I didn't see the sign." She pushes off the wall.

I've read where a character in a book says their blood drained in moments like this and I can tell you that's exactly what it feels like. *Whoosh,* from my arms, then, *whoosh,* from my legs. She's going to cremate me. I sniff back a whole morning full of tears and the sound bounces off the tile walls. I'm more than a doofus—I'm a snotty doofus.

Instead of hitting me, she cracks a grin. "You must be new here."

"I'm supposed to be in building two."

She takes another drag off the cigarette and exhales the smoke in a stream toward the ceiling. Then she runs her fingers under the faucet, pinches the lit end of the cigarette, and slides it into a makeup case from her backpack.

"C'mon," she says.

Obediently, I follow her out of the restroom and along the fenced perimeter of the yard. She stops at the far corner and points straight across.

"That's the library and behind it's the theater—seven and eight." She gestures to a building down from the library. "That's two."

"Oh, my gosh, thank you." For helping me. For not beating me up. "Thank you so much!"

She gives me that lopsided smile again. "Just stay out

of that bathroom." I nod vigorously. She takes a few steps backward. "Better get to class," she says. "Try not to smell like smoke!" She flashes a big smile and disappears.

★   ★   ★

The hardest part of being a new student is the five minutes between classes. While other girls joke around with one another, I pretend to be fascinated with my folders. You might remember me telling you about how Amanda and I came up with this idea. I wish Amanda were here right now. I'd be laughing and talking, too. I can't wait till after school to see her.

Business technology is my next class and it's in building 1. You'd think that's close to my first class in building 2, but American history is in the farthest end of building 2 and, I discover, business technology is in the farthest end of building 1. Even though I know where building 1 is, I'm still looking for room 118 when the bell rings.

Searching for my class, I realize the mark I will leave here will be the worn-out trail I make on the wood floor as I tread back and forth looking for 118. It's like my mother numbered this place.

Finally, I stop in front of a classroom with the door propped open. It's darker than the other classrooms. The metallic smell of hardware and electricity hums under my nose. Students at every desk sit behind open laptops, their faces reflecting bluish white light from the monitors.

"Oh, my gosh," I accidentally say out loud.

A few of the girls glance over and I shrink back. Then I spot Emily DeCamp, who sees me at the same time. Her eyes widen behind her glasses and her mouth makes a little O; I swear I hear her gasp. She straightens up in her chair. A kind of excitement takes over her expression, and she looks down at her desk with a wisp of a smile.

A girl not in uniform walks up to me and introduces herself. "Hi, you must be Hailee. I'm Ms. Reilly. Yes, I'm the teacher. I know I look young, but, class, how old am I?"

"A hundred and ninety-seven," they say in unison. I feel like an outsider as they giggle together at the class joke.

"Okay, okay," Ms. Reilly says. "Hailee, we need to get you up to speed on the project we're doing now. I've gone through your transcripts—you've got a pretty good background, but I'd still like to buddy you up with someone." She sweeps over the class.

Emily DeCamp raises her hand.

At least I know her. Ms. Reilly rearranges a few people so Emily and I can sit next to each other in the back, where a desk and laptop have already been set up for me.

"You *are* going to school here," she whispers as Ms. Reilly explains today's goals.

I shrug. I don't want to catch her enthusiasm.

The first thing Emily has me do is set up an e-mail address under the school's program. Then she sends me an e-mail: Want to sit with me at lunch? She doesn't look at me. I send her an e-mail back: Okay. She's sitting two feet away from me. I hear my e-mail ding her computer and I see her smile at her screen when she reads my answer.

Leaning toward me, she says, "We're making Web pages. Scoot your desk over, and I'll take you through mine."

Emily's Web page is for a fake business called Eat, Drink, and Read Books. Pretty good name and I tell her so. She clicks through the pages, one being Staff Favorites, in which the fake staff have picked their favorite books. Robert deGillyhoppy has selected *The City of Ember*. I point at the book cover on the screen. "I've read that!"

"Robert's read the whole series," she says.

"Me, too!" I forget for a second that Robert is really Emily.

Island of the Blue Dolphins, selected by Molly Toad. (Molly *Toad*!) "I love that book!"

Emily smiles.

Found, and the entire Missing series by Margaret Peterson Haddix—"Are you kidding me?" I can't believe this. "SHE'S MY FAVORITE AUTHOR!"

"Ahem," Ms. Reilly says. She doesn't clear her throat;

she says "ahem." "Girls? Let's try to contain our excitement for programming, okay?"

A quiet laughter bobs through the class, but it's okay because they're laughing with us, not at us, and Emily likes my favorite author and, "Have you read *Double Identity*?" I ask her.

Emily blinks with surprise. "I *own* that book!"

"Ahem." Except this time, it's a real throat clearing.

Emily buttons her mouth and faces forward.

★ ★ ★

I love you. I told you Mom's note would say that.

A girl named Cynthia sits with Emily and me at lunch. I ask Cyndi a few questions and she acts like I'm a mosquito buzzing around her ears. When she goes to get some napkins, Emily leans forward. "Don't call her Cyndi—she hates that."

Well, excuse me.

When Amanda and I sit at lunch, our conversation explodes like a bag of popcorn in the microwave, bursting and popping all over the place until the bag is puffy and fat. Cynthia, Emily, and I are cold fish on a plate—flat, quiet, and no one wants us.

Emily eats rice rolls with soy sauce she's brought from home. Dunk, bite, chew; dunk, bite, chew. Cynthia has a different method for her school pizza. She eats like a wood chipper, feeding one slice into her mouth and then another.

I eat my peanut butter and marshmallow sandwich. I swish my legs back and forth, developing a rhythm: *Swish, swisha. Swish, swisha.* I swing my shoulders to match my feet. In my head, a little song starts. Bo-ri-ring. Bo-ri-ring.

Cynthia lowers her pizza. "Can you sit still?"

"Can you speak Klingon?" I divide the fingers on one hand. " 'Live long and prosper.' "

Cynthia goes, "That's not Klingon; that's Vulcan."

Well!

The girl who was smoking in the bathroom cuts through the lunchroom with a couple of friends. People scoot their chairs or backpacks out of her way, and girls walking in the opposite direction pause to let her pass. She doesn't do anything to make this happen—it just does.

When the girl strolls past our table, her mouth hints at the lopsided grin she'd given me earlier. "Hey," she says, and she and her group keep walking, push open the doors, and go outside.

"You *know* her?" Cynthia holds a halfway buzzed slice of pizza in the air. Admiration colors her voice.

"Sort of." I don't want to say anything else about the girl, like how I caught her smoking or how she had a fight with her mom.

Emily lays a hand on her cheek. "That's Nikki Simms. She's popposite."

"What?"

"Popposite. Popular in the opposite way—like she's popular for being kind of bad." She dips her rice roll into the soy sauce, two hands up to her mouth, and munches it like a squirrel. "I submitted that word to Merriam-Webster."

"You can do that?"

"Right on their website."

I am amazed. Never before have I known a person who officially makes words for the dictionary. But she's more amazed with me.

"I can't believe she said hi to you. She's like . . ."

"Topular?"

"What's that?"

"Like, top of the popular people."

Emily DeCamp stares at me in wonder. "You just made up a word."

★　★　★

"And then Emily goes, 'You just made up a word.'" I've been on the phone for about forty-five minutes telling Amanda about my first day as a Magnolia girl. "So tomorrow in business technology, she's going to show me how to submit it to the dictionary."

"I didn't know you could—"

"Oh, my gosh, and did I tell you about the library— it's two stories and they have a Starbucks in it!"

"But you don't drink—"

"They would never have a Starbucks at Palm Middle!

Remember when the principal said no to a soda machine? And you should see the food in the cafeteria; it looked so good. Not like Palm Middle Worm Corn." This girl we don't really know sat down with her hot lunch and the grayish yellow corn niblets tumbled as a skinny dark worm climbed through them. The girl puked, probably the most exciting thing that happened that month, next to the worm, which became bigger and fatter each time we told the story.

Amanda doesn't laugh. She always laughs at Worm Corn.

"*How to Eat Fried Worms!*" I laugh, because that line's an inside joke for Amanda and me because we both read the book and saw the movie.

Silence.

"Hello-o?"

Amanda says in a small voice, "I kind of feel like you're insulting Palm Middle."

"No, I'm not! I'm telling you about Magnolia." The red-shouldered hawk does not destroy her nest.

Pause.

"They really have a Starbucks?"

"Yes!"

"That's so cool."

Together, we marvel over the outdoor Olympic-sized pool that I'll get to swim in for PE and then we debate the merits of having to wear a uniform and not having any boys in class.

"Speaking of boys," Amanda says, "I'm not supposed to tell you something."

"What? What is it?" I curl the phone closer to my face.

"Someone likes you but was afraid to tell you."

Someone *likes* me. Adrenaline races through me like a lightning strike. "Who?"

"I promised I wouldn't tell," Amanda says, "but it wouldn't be my fault if you guessed."

"Someone at our school?" I ask.

"Yessss." She drags it out.

A movie plays in my head of the boys crowding around me at lunch after the news got out about the lottery. I look at each of their faces, smiling at first, then sneering. I hope it's not one of them.

"I don't know. Just tell me."

"I can't!"

Squishing my eyes shut, I line the boys up and review my mental notes for them. I throw out a few names, including a couple of popular boys even though I know it can't be them, but I thought I would check just in case, but for every name I throw out, Amanda says nope.

"C'mon! Think! You always act like you don't notice him, but he has really pretty eyes, and he's funny . . . curly hair . . . people think he's cute . . . funny . . . curly hair—oh, my gosh, I can't believe you aren't guessing this—*Rabbit*!"

I gasp. "Tanner Law?"

"Finally!" she roars. "Just remember, you guessed; I didn't tell you."

She talks about other stuff and I say "uh-huh" and "oh" when her voice tells me to, but I'm stuck at *Tanner Law likes me.*

"What did he say about me?" I interrupt whatever she's saying that I wasn't exactly listening to.

"He sat with me at lunch today and said he always thought you were pretty, but he never said anything to you because he thought you didn't like him that way."

Even though she can't see me, I nod. "What did you say?"

"I told him lots of girls think he's hot."

"But what did you say about me?"

Silence.

It's funny how a bunch of no words at all makes you press the phone against your ear even harder and pace around your room like a lion in its cage.

"Hel-lo," I say. "Amanda? Amanda?"

I want to reach through the phone and pluck her vocal cords. "Amanda! What did you tell Tanner about me?"

"I said . . . like . . . I don't know what I said. I wasn't sure if you liked him like that. You never talk about him."

Hmm, true. I didn't know he liked me when he said *Rabbit* the day I wore my green shirt. I mean, Tanner

Law—I remember when he used to suck his thumb. Still, an unfamiliar feeling of lightness rises in my chest. *A boy likes me.* I guess he's okay. It kind of changes things to know he likes me.

Chapter 11

All through supper, I try to decide if I like Tanner Law. Dad offers a nickel for my thoughts, which used to be a penny, but he's adjusted it for inflation. "Nothing," I say.

"And your first day went well?" Mom asks for the sixteenth time.

Why does she keep asking me if my first day went well? You know she only wants to hear me say yes. What if I told her the truth; what if I told her, *Well, the building numbers are all mixed up, so I got lost on campus; I was tardy to most of my classes; I knocked over a cheerleader; and when I went into a bathroom to cry, there was a girl in there smoking. How was your day?*

I pretend I can't answer because my mouth is full. And it is, but not with words she wants to hear.

Dad touches my arm. "Maybe this will cheer you

up." He smiles at Mom, then me. "After supper, I'm taking you out for a new bike!"

"Yes!" I punch the air in a victory pose. The first thing on my list of Things I Need! Finally, the lottery is paying off. I shovel the chicken casserole into my mouth like an engineer trying to keep the train's fire going. I glug the milk and slam the glass down. Screeching back my chair, I jump and wave air pom-poms. "Ready!"

"Raa!" Libby says. She wants to be like me.

"Give me a minute," Dad says.

"Hurry up, Da-ad, hurry up, BOOM! BOOM! Hurry up, Da-ad, hurry up, BOOM! BOOM!" I stamp my feet on the *boom boom* part.

"Settle down," Mom says, putting more carrot bits onto Libby's tray.

Dad says, "Put your shoes on."

My arms make a high V. "Yay!"

"Aaaee!" Libby, getting in on it. Orange carrotballs fly across the kitchen.

My shoes are on, my hopes are up, my dad's still eating. Quietly, I sing, "Hurry up, Da-ad, hurry up, *boom! boom!*" I whisper that last part.

Mom gives me the evil eye, but I see a twinkle in it.

I whistle the tune, singing the words in my head as I pace in laps through the kitchen, living room, and dining room.

The sun is setting by the time Dad's ready to leave.

Bright pink strokes and swirls of orange look like watercolors against the darkening blue sky. Dad lifts the garage door, and as he crosses the threshold, one strand of the bougainvillea laces itself around him. If I didn't know better, I'd think it was hugging him. He picks it off one pricker at a time, careful to not break the vine.

"Remind me to tie that thing up or chop it down," he says, pretending I don't know that bougainvillea is his pride and joy.

When Dad and I finally head into a sports center, I sprint straight to the bikes in back. The salesman there has tattoos and rings stuck in his face. He points out different bicycles to Dad, explaining their features, blah, blah, blah, ohmygosh.

A girl's bike near the end flashes its glittery newness at me. The white handgrips beg my fingers to grab them. I can practically feel the energy coursing through its wires. I walk over and slide my hands over the chrome. "Can I try this one out?" I call to the salesman.

"Go ahead," he says.

At first, I hop on and pedal the bike slowly, as if we're taking a Sunday ride, but somewhere between the scooters and the bathing suits, the power of the bike overtakes me. I pump like mad down the linoleum path that cuts around the store. "Beep! Beep!" I yell at a man walking too slowly. "Beep! Beep!" Old lady. "Beep! Beep!" I fly past Dad and the salesman.

"Slow down!" Dad hollers.

I force the pedals faster. My feet are pistons; sparks fly off the chain. People leap out of the way.

Dad flags me, but I race past him. I'm on spin cycle. I blur past the tents, the baseball bats, and the grills, speed by the cashiers, the shoes, and come up to the bikes again.

Dad steps into my path, but I press into the wind.

"Beep! Beep!"

"Hailee!"

"BEEP! BEEP!"

"HAILEE!"

My feet backpedal until I remember the handbrakes. I squeeze them hard. The tires squeal and lose their grip, sending me and the bike into a long, turning skid that ends in a slide along the floor.

When I get up and roll the silver bike back to its spot, Dad and the salesman stare at me. They are amazed. But as I get close, I see a vein popping out on Dad's forehead, a vein so rarely seen, his heart probably doesn't even know about it. His teeth slide back and forth over each other, chewing back words he's too mad to say.

I glance at the salesman. The stud in his eyebrow lifts with admiration.

"How many speeds does this one have?" I ask. I have used only one: faster than the speed of light.

"Fourteen," he says. His lip ring twinkles.

Amanda's has twelve. "I'll take it."

When we get into the van and buckle up, Dad starts

the motor but doesn't drive. "Hailee," he starts and bends his head.

I'm about to get the biggest talking-to he's ever given. First the vein, now the serious voice. Probably a punishment, too. He hangs over the steering wheel in the dark, engine rumbling, then he shakes his head.

He starts laughing. I start laughing. Then he laughs louder, which makes me laugh harder, and in between laughing, he gasps for air and tries to say, "Beep! Beep!" which makes us crack up, our mouths open and our shoulders shaking with laughter so hard, it's silent.

That night, I smile in my bed thinking about it. Overall, things are going pretty well. My first day at school and I already have someone to hang with—Emily; Amanda was properly impressed with my Magnolia stories; someone likes me; and best of all, I got the Treads Silver Flash 151 bicycle with fourteen speeds. Even my cheery maple seems to have perked up, decorated on the tips with moonlit buds. Soon it will have new leaves.

Chapter 12

. . . .

My second Magnolia day starts with crying and screaming, but not mine.

Mom bought Libby a fancy new car seat, but judging
by the way the windows are trying not to crack, I'd say
Libby does not like it. She howls and thrashes against
her five-point harness baby seat belt.

"Can you make her be quiet?" Her shrieks are curling my eyebrow hairs. This can't possibly be the best
way to start my day.

Stress pours out of Mom's mouth. "I'm driving right
now. Can you do something?"

If I twist too much, I'll wrinkle my smooth Magnolia uniform. "It's because you've got her sitting backward. I don't see why she needed a new car seat anyway."
The old one wasn't even that old; Mom bought it from
a daycare yard sale only a year ago.

"I thought it would be nice, just like you getting a new bike."

"She doesn't know—she's a baby! And besides, she hates it."

"It's safer for her. I've been talking with the ladies at church and everyone's using these backward-facing ones now. So hate it or not, she's safer."

Safe, shrieking Libby wails in the backseat. I press my hands so hard over my ears, if my head were a watermelon, I'd burst it. Over Libby's crying, I yell, "Did I have a car seat like that?"

"No." Mom checks her mirrors before turning into the entrance for school. The van has a sticker now, so we wait as the gate opens automatically for us.

Libby's going to grow up spoiled.

When Mom stops at the dropoff for Magnolia, I recognize the expensive car in front of us—Nikki Simms. The mother's head has a cell phone pasted to one ear. Her fingers toodley-doo to Nikki, and she's laughing into the phone when she pulls away.

Nikki strolls the Magnolia path alone.

"Honey?" Mom says.

"Oh." I unbuckle.

Mom leans over the console, but I bend my head, letting her give my hair a quick peck, then I check the back windshield to make sure no one saw that.

Babies like moving cars, but boy, do they hate parked

vans. Libby grabs at the air and screams. I get my stuff together and finger the door handle.

"Have a good day!" Mom yells over the squalling.

Pencils fall out of an unzipped pocket, and spiral notebooks slosh from a different pouch when I bend down to pick up the pencils. The power of Libby's howling scrambles my brain; I keep dropping things. Then she ramps up, her wailing pressing against the insides of the van. The doors and windows strain not to crack. This is a Category 4 tantrum—one-hundred-and-fifty-miles-an-hour shrieks and floods of tears.

I'm sweaty and rattled when I tumble onto the sidewalk. Libby delivers a roar so full of unhappiness and dissatisfaction, I slam the van door fast so none of it leaks out.

Poor Mom. Poor *me*!

After they leave, my day is immediately easier. I know where to go and I get there on time. I try to work in some of my poses as I walk: *over the shoulder,* which I use after tripping on a sidewalk crack; *runway walk*, which is extending your neck and holding your head straight like you've got a string pulling you up, except my heavy backpack makes me hunch forward a little; and *Oh! I can't find something*, which is where I root through my backpack pretending to search for an assignment because the bell hasn't rung yet and we're not supposed to go into the classrooms until then.

After lunch, Emily introduces me to the media specialist, Mrs. Weston, who seems impressed when I start listing all the books I've read since Christmas. When she hands me the sign-up sheet for the Library Club, I see that I'll be the fourth member. I hesitate with the pen for a moment. Why are only three other people listed? Are Library Club members losers?

Panic buzzes in my head. I'm in a new school, but I'm at the same place—dorksville. The uniforms make us look alike, but they don't disguise our statuses. How is that possible? Emily's okay, but I can already see that people think she's a nerd. *And I'm hanging around with her.* I cap the pen shut and lay it on the desk.

Mrs. Weston says, "Oh, you're going to fit right in. Sometimes we read the same book and have group discussion; sometimes we'll watch the movie after we read the book and talk about which one was better." Okay, I do like doing that kind of stuff. "And sometimes, I pull you out of class to read books to our kindergarteners."

It does sound fun. I uncap the pen, hold my writing hand over the form, but I can't make myself sign.

Mrs. Weston taps a blank line on the form. "Right there. And then one of your parents' names and a phone number where they can be reached." I like the way she does her hair. It's kind of flippy.

Mrs. Weston smiles. I sort of smile back; then I realize she's waiting for me to fill out the form.

Three members.

I don't want to be a loser. I glance down at the sign-up sheet, and then I make my first important decision at Magnolia.

Chapter 13

· · · · · · · · · · · · · ·

"Mom! I joined the Library Club!" I say, climbing into Mom's van after school. Libby naps in her backward seat. Thank God.

I almost didn't join. But then my brain said, *You know you love this library. Wood floors, curved banisters, green comfy chairs—and don't forget the Starbuck's!* My brain was right. I decided the people who hadn't joined the Library Club were the true losers and I added my name to the list.

The Silver Flash waits for me like a horse in its stall. The old red bike leans against the wall like an old man on a cane. For a second, I feel sorry for it. It was a loyal bike and even though it *is* the ugliest tomato red with rust to match, and sounds like a cat hacking up hairballs, cost the same as a school lunch, and doesn't have hand brakes or speeds, it served me well. But like I said, that feeling lasts only a second. The Silver Flash is so much easier to love.

I would pay more than a dollar and a pack of Smarties to ride the Silver Flash. But I will take the high road. Amanda can ride it for free.

"Really?" She is humbled by my generosity. She shoots me a serious glance and goes, "I'll be careful."

We're riding to Matthew's game at the high school this afternoon. I've got money in my pocket and plans to spend it—the snack bar at the baseball fields has just about everything. I sit on Amanda's driveway, the cement rough and warm against my skin, and watch her ride my bike. My freckles start to get hot. I wish they would connect; then I would be really tan.

The garage door roars open and I shriek.

Running footsteps, then, "What?"

I look up into Matthew's face and feel mine turn a million shades of I'm-so-embarrassed.

He tilts his head. His shaggy, curly hair falls to the side in waves. "You okay?"

I nod dumbly.

Somehow, in his black jersey and gray baseball pants, he's taller; his eyes are greener; the muscles in his arms are bigger. He leans down, brings his face closer to mine. My heart pounds. My eyes close.

He swats a lovebug off my cheek.

"You better move off the driveway," he says, pulling open the driver's side door of their van. Matthew has his learner's permit. "We're about to back up. I'd hate to ruin my perfect driving record!" He climbs in.

I stand, move into the grass. Nerves jangle across my cheek where he brushed it.

Mrs. Burns comes out. "Hi, Hailee! Where's Amanda?"

I rotate like a zombie and point. Mrs. Burns shades her eyes and squints. "Okay. See you at the game!"

Matthew blares the horn as he passes Amanda, who shouts, "Matthew!" Then to me, "I hate when he does that!" as she rides up the driveway. "It startles me."

I think of his face so close to mine, his fingertips touching my cheek, and even though it was a swat instead of a stroke, my heart knocks around in its cage like a super-bouncy ball. "He startled me, too."

"This bike," she says, leaning it back to me, "is *nice*."

"Yours is nice, too," I say, because it *is* nice, for a bike with only twelve speeds.

I swear Amanda is secretly racing me as we wind through town to the field. Anytime I get a little ahead of her, she catches up and then I have to pedal harder to keep my position. Black, mushy lovebugs flit across the road searching for girlfriends. They splat against my fenders, dotting the Treads Silver Flash 151 with their buggy guts.

Stupid lovebugs. Stupid, stupid lovebugs.

★   ★   ★

Amanda and I mill around the fields with our cotton-candy cones. Boys tower over us with their high school bodies, and girls their age pretend not to see them, but then there they go, flipping their hair and giggling even louder until the boys pass. Then they huddle and laugh again.

We take our time getting to the bleachers. The broiling smell of hamburgers on the grill drifts over the sidewalks and we filter through the people aiming to get their food before the game starts. Music pumps over the loudspeakers; every bass note vibrates inside me. Some people we say hi to and some we don't.

"Oh, gosh," Amanda says.

"What?"

She gestures with her cotton-candy cone toward the bleachers.

Some of Palm Middle School's popular people sit on the first two benches. Avoid! Avoid! My eyes detect an opening on the other side, but then someone rolls up in a wheelchair, closing the gap. Old people sit in camp chairs right in front, forming a scowling fence of too many years in the sun and the deep creases to prove it. They look like alligator wrestlers.

"Over here, honey," Amanda's mom shouts and waves from the back row of the bleachers.

Some of the popular girls wrinkle their eyebrows, then titter.

Amanda covers her face with her hand. "Oh, my God. Why does she have to be so embarrassing?"

It would be wrong to disturb the man in the wheelchair, and just plain scary to bother the alligator wrestlers. The only way to our seats is through the popular people. Amanda realizes this the same time I do, and she trudges reluctantly toward that side.

These girls don't look up or move their knees or do anything a normal polite person would do to let you get by.

Amanda shifts uncomfortably in front of them as I stand behind her. "Um . . . excuse me?"

The two closest girls lean apart ever so slightly without a glance in our direction.

"Thank you," Amanda says and slips through.

One of the girls rolls her eyes.

For a second, I'm afraid to pass through their invisible barbed-wire fence, but what else can I do?

"Ex*cuse* me," one of them says as I follow Amanda's path.

"Oh, I'm"—about to say I'm sorry, but then something overtakes me. Something powerful and strong, because though they are the popular people, they're not *my* popular people anymore.

I fix my face into a happy expression. "Oh, hi, Maggie! Hi, Natalie!"

Their faces go into shock. A mere citizen has broken the rules by speaking to them. The fence goes down. I rattle my way up the bleachers, stomping on each step and calling out names as I pass. "Hi, Morgan! Hi, Kayla! Hi, Stephanie!"

"Hailee!" says Stephanie, whose corn-silk-colored hair goes almost to her waist and has been the envy of every girl since kindergarten. She twists her whole body around. "Don't you go to Magnolia now? How is it?"

Stephanie Mills is asking me a question. Hanging around with Morgan and Kayla and sometimes even Megan, Stephanie isn't supposed to be nice. She's supposed to push people in the hallways and call them losers. I check my mental notes. Nope, no record of Stephanie Mills doing anything at all like that. I may have to open up a new folder for this strain of popular beings.

Her smile and open eyes wait for my answer. Morgan and Kayla stare up at me, but their mouths are forward slashes—grimaces that disapprove of Stephanie talking to me.

"Magnolia is great!" I settle next to Amanda, who'd better shut her mouth before bees fly in there after the cotton candy. Remembering that Stephanie is in drama, I add, "They have a whole building just for theater classes."

"Wow," she says in a respectful tone. "I would love that."

I smile because I can't think of anything else to say.

Kayla tugs on Stephanie's arm.

"Well, good luck," Stephanie says to me.

"Thanks!" I wait for her to turn back to her friends before I whip around to Amanda with my oh-my-gosh face.

Amanda's got hers on, too. "I can't believe you talked to them!"

"I can't believe I did, either!" I can't believe Stephanie talked back. She's never talked to me before. But actually, *I've* never talked to *her*, either. I guess I've never looked at it that way.

The game starts and it's kind of boring until it's Matthew's turn to bat. He takes a couple of practice swings, then steps up to the plate. The pitcher nods to the catcher, then winds up and burns one into the mitt.

"Stee-rike one!"

Matthew steps back, loosens his shoulders, and readies himself. He swings hard. The sound of the bat hitting the ball sends all the players into motion.

"Foul ball! Strike two!"

Matthew's coach yells from the dugout, "You're swinging at high balls! Don't give it to them!"

"Come on, Matthew!" a girl shouts.

Amanda and I lean over to see who's rooting for her brother. Halfway across the bleachers, a girl whose prettiness is in the middle sits with her eyes fastened on Matthew.

"Who's that?" I ask, but Amanda shrugs, stuffs a knot of cotton candy into her mouth, and focuses on the game. I perform a laser scan on the girl. Age: same as Matthew's. Rank: I'm guessing normal person, since she's sitting with only one other girl, probably her best friend. Prettiness: a little more than in the middle, now that I look at her.

She leans forward and bites her lip as if his next swing will decide the fate of the entire galaxy, including planets we haven't even discovered yet and all their moons.

Matthew bends his knees, brings the bat behind his shoulder. I hold my breath as the pitcher lets go a fast one, and then *crack*! Matthew's off! His feet turn up red clouds of clay as he rounds first base and stops at second. Everyone cheers. I spy on the girl, and she's clapping and smiling with her friend.

Amanda's finished her cotton candy and hands both of our sticky wands to her mother. "Thank you!" Amanda says.

"Oh, brother." Her mom smirks.

The next batter hits Matthew to third.

"What're the popular people like at Magnolia?" Amanda asks. Points at popular heads. "I still can't believe you said hi to them."

"I'm already friends with the most popular girl in school," I say, maybe even loud enough for Palm populars to hear me. "Her name's Nikki."

The catcher misses the next pitch. Matthew starts

down the third-base line until the catcher charges him back. The other coach yells, "When he does that, when he starts to run again, FINISH HIM!"

I'm not even a player and *I*'m scared to move.

"Matt!" Matthew's coach stands near third base. He taps the brim of his baseball cap, touches his nose, tugs two times on one ear, and slides his fingertips across his stomach. Matthew nods—he has decoded the secret message.

Every single back on our side straightens; all pairs of eyes lock onto the field; hands clasp and fingers touch lips. As the catcher crouches, Matthew leads off. He is not afraid.

Everyone is silent.

The next batter drives the ball across the infield. The shortstop catches it, stumbles, and the ball shoots into the grass. Matthew sprints home and, as the outfielders chase and drop the ball, Matthew's teammates cross the plate right behind him. Our side lights up like fireworks, shooting from our seats, whistling and cracking high-fives. The girl cheering for Matthew raises her arms over her head and claps hard.

The visiting coach clutches the chain-link wall of his dugout. "East Panthers!" A colonel commanding his troops. "If they start that merry-go-round again, SHUT THEM DOWN!" He could win wars all by himself with his yelling. It's his words, his loudness, the granite set of his face when he blasts out his orders.

I glance at the scoreboard and see we're down by six runs. Maybe our coach should start yelling, too.

The game goes on and Amanda presses me for more details about Nikki. What does she look like, how old is she, does she wear makeup—I answer all her questions as though I've known Nikki all my life instead of just two days.

When Matthew comes to bat again, he strikes out. He jogs to the dugout with a determined look on his face. I can't imagine what it must feel like to strike out in front of all these people. But as he passes the next batter, his teammates clap him on the shoulder or say "Good try."

Even when the game is over and we've lost, Matthew is fine. He jokes around with friends as Amanda and I walk our bikes alongside Matthew and their mom through the parking lot. As he opens the trunk of the van and throws his bag in, that girl and her friend catch up.

"Matthew, hi!"

Matthew whips around, sees her, and I swear he looks more scared for a second than he ever did out on that field. But he covers it quickly. "Shana!" He closes the distance between them. "I didn't think you were coming."

Swinging her shoulders, she says, "I told you I would, silly." She playfully nudges his arm.

Scanning . . . scanning . . . Scan complete: prettier up

close, but not stuck-up pretty; voice good (not that stupid singsong, high-pitched tone some girls suddenly use when a boy they like is near); giggling—none. She even says hello to Amanda and me.

"Okay, girls," Mrs. Burns says to us. "Better start riding before it gets dark."

Matthew and Shana keep talking.

"Bye, Mom," Amanda says. "Good game, Matteew!"

I don't even think he hears her.

As we pedal home, I ask Amanda if Matthew's allowed to have girlfriends.

"Beats me," she says.

He asked her to come to the game. *To watch him*, I realize. That's how it works when you're a teenager.

"If he runs," Amanda bellows, "finish him!"

"Shut him down!" I crow. I wonder if Matthew and Shana will become boyfriend and girlfriend. Does your cheek tingle when any boy touches it, or only when certain boys touch it? I don't think my cheek would tingle if Tanner Law flicked a bug off me.

Some of the popular girls have boyfriends. They hold the boys' hands in the hallways, then talk about them in class. And even before boyfriends, they acted like they knew something the rest of us didn't. Except maybe Stephanie. I mean, she *is* popular, but she acts like a normal person. Also, that nice cheerleader I bumped into on my first day at Magnolia. But then there're the rest of them, the ones who think they're better, which I don't get because Morgan has a wart on her left hand that has a brown dot on it. I'm not saying warts make a person bad—I'm just saying how can you act like you're all that when your left hand looks like the tip of a witch's nose?

Amanda and I don't have any warts. Also, we are nicer. For instance, I hold the door open until the person behind me grabs it. Once I was holding the door, and instead of falling behind and taking the door for herself, Kayla and another girl walked straight through as if I were their servant. Ladies of leisure, as my mom would say.

"SHUT THEM DOWN! Shut them all down!" I howl. Amanda's a couple feet in front of me. I knock my bike into a different speed to catch up.

She stands on her pedals and pumps even faster. "You're out!" she yells.

I'm not out. I'm not a loser. I whip the Silver Flash into a frenzy, and we tear up the road, Amanda and I, fast as cheetahs and cracking up all the way home.

Chapter 14

· · · · · · · · · · · · · · · ·

The tardy bell has already rung for fifth-period history when the door swings open.

Mrs. Fuller crosses her arms. "Well, Miss Simms, we're glad you could join us."

Miss Simms? I strain around the big head of the girl sitting diagonal from me to see who's come in.

It *is* her.

Nikki Simms is in my history class.

Mrs. Fuller's stare is so sharp it could cut down trees, but Nikki is not affected by it. She strolls to a desk in the back row. She thumps her backpack on the floor. She rattles her paper, creaks open her book, and pops her gum.

"Miss Simms?"

Nikki stops chewing.

Mrs. Fuller raises her eyebrows.

Into a piece of notebook paper, Nikki spits her gum,

then walks to the front of the class and throws it out. After Nikki sits down, Mrs. Fuller drops her arms.

"What were we chatting about? Oh, yes." Her voice takes on the quality of a game show host. "The structures in Rome represent the most superb architecture aside from the pyramids in the ancient world." She waves her arm. "When you get off the plane, the Pantheon is to your right."

Nikki lifts her hand.

"Yes, Miss Simms?"

Nikki clears her throat. "I believe the Pantheon is to your *left* as you get off the plane."

The class snickers. Mrs. Fuller pinches her mouth. "Miss Simms. Do you have a clinic pass or excuse for your absences this week?"

"I'll make sure you get one, Mrs. Fuller."

Mrs. Fuller's thin lips form a straight line. "Well, then. Enough chatting—let's get on with today's lesson."

I risk glancing backward. Nikki Simms looks right at me. Her blue eyes are wide and innocent, but the corner of her mouth lifts in a joke, a joke between her and me. If my mom had heard Mrs. Fuller talking about getting off the plane in Rome, she would've called her Lady Fuller. *Full of herself.* Ooh—good one. If I were sitting next to Nikki, I'd pass it to her on a note and she'd smile when she read it.

Civil War: Brother against Brother is the chapter we are to silently read.

It describes how when the Civil War started, not everyone agreed as to people having different stations in life simply due to the color of their skin or the country of their origin. "Some people ardently believed in the words of our Declaration," the book reads, "which states that all men are created equal. And these people were willing to fight to make that equality a reality. Brothers, relatives, and friends found themselves facing each other from opposite lines on the battlefield."

I don't think I could do that, war or not. I couldn't hurt my sister or Amanda even if the president himself asked me to.

★ ★ ★

"What do you think of Mrs. Fuller?" I ask Emily as we push the book cart through the library, my first Library Club meeting after school.

"She's okay."

"Some people think she's kind of snobby."

Emily shrugs. "She's okay."

Dewey Decimal Does It Right! A poster cheers us on. Dewey Decimal is a book with arms and legs, huge eyes and a great big smile. You can tell he loves the library by his enthusiastic strut and the way his elbow is cocked, as if he's about to say, *Oh, boy!*

We're shelving fiction, which is easy, because it's in alphabetical order by author's last name. The only time I don't know what to do is when the author has two names, such as Margaret Peterson Haddix or Frances Hodgson Burnett. Do they go under the first last name or the second last name? I don't want to look stupid by asking Emily.

What would Dewey do . . . what would Dewey do? I glance up at the poster.

Dewey would want readers to find the books. I place half the copies in the first last name area and the other half in the second last name area.

Done with that job, Emily and I have twenty minutes to kill. The other two members of the club, whose names I don't remember, are upstairs, lucky them. They got to file the nonfiction books and now they get to polish all the gleaming honey-colored banisters and handrails. The lemony smell wafts its way down to the main floor.

The librarian suggests that we silently read, but I already do that at home. Clubs are supposed to be exciting. Like, we're in the Library Club, we should be making plans to visit the Library of Congress, or have a famous author visit us, or even take a field trip to the downtown library.

I slap the table, waking everybody up. "I know what we should do!" I say to Emily. "We should make a display of staff favorites like on your website!"

Emily's glasses magnify the look of delight in her eyes. "I always wanted to do that!"

Mrs. Weston, the media specialist, says, "I've had the same idea!"

Even the girls upstairs call out their agreement.

All of a sudden we are in motion. We quickly declare some rules: each person picks out one book, except Mrs. Weston, who picks out one for each grade. We'll put up new favorites once a month. It takes all four of us girls to lug an unused bookcase from behind the main desk to the front. While we're doing that, Mrs. Weston prints out fancy name cards that she'll post over our selections.

So many books—I don't want to leave any out. I run around and end up with a pile of twelve books that I cut down to three by closing my eyes and pressing one fingertip to three different spines. I'm excited over my selections. Bright, colorful covers say, *Hey, I'm fun. Check me out!* One has a cat on the cover and hairclips because the girl in the book makes the cat wear fancy hairdos. My books are a ribbon of pink hijinks.

"Everyone will see what we've picked!" Emily says, dropping her own collection on the table near the display shelf. "This is going to be great!"

I'm holding one of my girly-girl books in midair when I play back what Emily just said. "Everyone will see what we've picked." Everyone. Everyone means Nikki. I look at my selections through Nikki's eyes and see that I've picked cotton candy and rainbows.

Nikki will think I'm a little girl. She might not say "hey" to me anymore.

Grabbing my choices, I quietly let them fall into the

book drop so I don't have to bother with them, then I search my brain and the aisles for just the right one to put under my name. Everyone will see what we've picked. This isn't just staff favorites anymore, I realize; by selecting the right books, I could be a new, cooler Hailee.

What books would Cool Hailee read? I pass up wizards and boyfriend problems and a few skulls. Cool Hailee reads cool books—nothing sweet, nothing with grandmas in it, and nothing pink. Cool Hailee also doesn't read the books everyone talks about because Cool Hailee doesn't follow the crowd.

I quickly exhaust fiction A through G. Up front, Mrs. Weston coos over Emily's selection. I'd better hurry. I round the corner to the Hs. *The Outsiders*! S. E. Hinton, who lots of people think is a guy because that's how cool this book is but really the author is Susan Eloise Hinton.

"Girls, we need to finish up or they'll lock us in!"

I grab Ponyboy, Soda, and Johnny off the shelf and hand *The Outsiders* to Mrs. Weston as she scoots us out. The four of us trade titles, talk about our selections as we head to the front of the school to wait for our rides. Everyone else pulls out a phone and calls or texts their moms.

"Do you need to borrow my phone?" one of the other girls asks when she sees me just standing there.

"She's probably already on her way," I say, and magically Mom appears. The van loops through the parking lot and squeals to a stop in front of us. I cringe at the squeaks, the rust, and the fact that my mom was so punctual, the first one here. As I slowly rise, another van pulls up behind her.

Mom gets out wearing her pink shirt with bleach spots and her cut-off shorts; she's carrying Libby, whose after-nap hair is teased high and sticks out at the sides. The other mom pops out in tan capris, a sleeveless white blouse, and hair and makeup that look like she ought to be out shopping on Park Avenue. Her delicate French-manicured fingernails twinkle as she waves. Mom looks like she's dressed to clean this lady's house.

I put my head down and hurry to the car. "Bye, Emily," I say quickly, but it's too late. The baby magnet has drawn in all the other girls. They surround my mom and fuss over Libby, trying to make her laugh, and she delivers. Story of my life. I think Libby's cute and everything, but sometimes I want to keep things just for myself. When people make a big deal over Libby, it's like they totally forget about me.

When Mom finally gets us on our way home, I say, "Were you doing laundry or something before you came?"

"Just having a snack," she says, still enjoying how everyone mollycoddled Libby.

"I mean, it looks like you ran out of clothes to wear."

"What are you talking about? I always wear these clothes."

"I know." I can't help but take a sideways look and

compare her to my mental notes on the other mom. "Maybe you should get some new stuff, like capris or some nicer tops."

"What? You don't like what I have on?" Her voice is jokey.

Mine is not. "It looks a little . . ." I'm hoping she'll get the idea so I don't have to finish this sentence. "Did you see the other . . ."

Mom's tone changes. "Did I see the other what, Hailee?"

"The moms here dress differently." There. I said it. I'm afraid to look at her.

"Well!" She clicks the blinker on. "Maybe the other mothers are afraid of breaking a nail. You're getting a little hoity-toity, aren't you?"

Her lips wrinkle together. Her silence fills the car like an airbag and I'm pushed against my seat, unable to move because of the pressure.

You sent me here, I want to tell her. The way she juts her jaw is a sign: Warning! Do Not Proceed! Warning! But I can't help myself. "*You* said Palm Middle wasn't good enough. I'm not getting hoity-toity; I'm trying to be better now and you should, too." I quote from the school video we watched on the tour. " 'Magnolia isn't just a school; it's a lifestyle.' "

Mom's grip on the steering wheel tightens. In a low voice, she says, "I've done everything I could to give you opportunities I didn't have—"

"I didn't ask to change schools," I say. "You put me in a rich school, then you criticize the other mothers."

"No, I don't."

"Ladies of leisure," I say. "Afraid of breaking a nail. You call Mrs. Burns something and you don't even know the work she does all day."

"I'm sick of you talking about these other people like they're something special. Do you know—"

I whip around so quickly, my seat belt locks. "They *are* special. They're special to me. And just so you know, Amanda's mom *never* calls *you* 'Lady Richardson.'"

Mom stares straight ahead as she drives. I sit in the stew of her anger—what I thought was her anger—until she says, "I'm sorry. I shouldn't call Mrs. Burns that."

"You shouldn't call any of them that," I say.

The very last molecule of anything positive drains from her face. She looks tired all of a sudden. "That's enough, Hailee, okay?" But her voice is quiet and has no energy behind it.

We ride in silence the rest of the way home.

Chapter 15

. . . .

"Eeeew!" With gloved hands, I pick up a snot rag caught in the weeds along Culver Street. I never realized how many litterbugs live in Palm Hill until I agreed to help Amanda clean up two blocks of Culver. It's her first community project; she has to do at least three to be considered for the Compass Club next year.

Amanda throws some fast food wrappers into the trash bag. "Thank you so much for helping me."

At Magnolia, we're required to be involved in extracurricular activities and one sport. The Library Club is my activity, and I came to Magnolia too late for sports, which, even though I don't have a favorite, would beat trash picking any day.

Soda cans and beer bottles pop up like prairie dogs along the side of the road. Some of the bottles are smashed, so I pick up different-colored shards the same way I pick up sea shells—carefully. Dragonflies helicopter above us. Lovebugs pepper the air. I keep an eye out for fire ants.

Candy bar wrappers, potato chip bag, a sneaker. How does someone lose one sneaker? Were they running and a shoe fell off and they were like, *Oh, well, I can't be stopping for a sneaker.*

As we ramble along the roadside, picking up things people know they shouldn't be throwing out their car windows, we talk about Palm Middle. Amanda's been eating with other people. I'm glad, because I wouldn't want her to be alone. We chat about her new lunch table, which includes Becca and Tanner Law.

"So," Amanda asks, "do you like him?"

Pile of dog poop. *That* is not litter and I am *not* picking it up.

"Do I like who?"

Amanda sighs, all exasperated. "Do you like Tanner?"

I completely forgot to think about him. I shrug my shoulders. "I don't know yet. Is that what he talks to you about?" I do like the idea of being on someone's mind.

"Well, he talks about other stuff, too," Amanda says.

The sheen on her arms is speckled with dirt and something purple. Wisps frizz out from her ponytail, sticking to her red face. She will be tan tomorrow. I will be burned with more freckles. Or I will be less white with darker freckles. Either way, I'm frying. My skin crisps like bread in a toaster.

The whole time we work, cars whiz by, there being no stop sign on this stretch, but then a white convertible slows as it passes. The brake lights flash, and the car backs up.

Nikki Simms leans out from the backseat. Darkened eyelashes, shiny lips. An older, bored version of her sits in the front and some guy is driving.

"What are you doing?" Nikki asks.

I'm standing here, covered in sweat and garbage, and wearing rubber gloves. Just stamp *Loser* on my forehead.

"Community service." She'll never be my friend after this.

Amanda steps up. She knows who I'm talking with, I can tell, and now I wish I hadn't let her believe Nikki and I were such good friends. She says, "I'm applying for the Compass Club, and one of the projects was neighborhood cleanup. Hailee's helping me."

Nikki gives me the once-over. "Cool."

"Are you done yet?" the older girl asks. She's got to be Nikki's sister. She takes a drag from a cigarette and flicks the ashes into the gutter.

Nikki drains a soda can and holds it out. "Allow me to contribute to the cause."

I can't tell if we're being made fun of or not, so I trudge up with the trash bag and she tosses the can.

Amanda moves right in. "Are you Nikki?"

I could die right now, except I see a trace of Nikki's lopsided grin. She could've beaten me up, but instead she helped me. People move out of the way for her. The Pantheon is to your left.

A long plume of smoke pipes from the front of the car. "I'm getting hot," the sister says.

The guy starts to pull away.

"Wait!" Nikki yells and the car stops. "Want to go for a ride?"

Nikki Simms wants to know if I, Hailee Richardson, want to ride in a convertible with her. I glance at Amanda. Nikki picks up on this immediately and turns her magnet eyes on Amanda. "Want to?"

Amanda's shocked. Nothing this good has ever happened to us. Besides winning the lottery, of course.

Hesitation.

How many times has a popular person invited us to do something with her? Um, *never*—until now.

"C'mon, Amanda." I try to keep the eagerness out of my voice, but I feel the pleading in my eyes.

Amanda responds with the slightest movement of her head. "We don't have permission." Her answer makes me feel the way the claw machine at Denny's does when I've finally gotten hold of the best prize and just before I move it over the chute, the prize slips from the claw and I walk away empty-handed.

"Taxi's running," the guy says.

Nikki pulls up on his headrest. "Can we take them around the block?"

"Whatever."

I shoot a hopeful glance at Amanda, but she shakes her head.

She can't do this to me. This ride, right now, could make or break me at Magnolia. I can't *not* do it. "It's only around the block. Please." I add that last part with a look on my face that tells her, *Ohmygosh, Amanda, we have to do this*, but I guess I didn't get the message across because she says I can go if I want to, but she is staying right here.

Bored Older Sister speaks. "Make up your mind, chain gang."

Amanda presses her lips together.

Nikki beams like an adventure waiting to happen. I can collect trash any old day. Nikki picks up on my thoughts because she scoots over and asks her sister to get the door. Bored Older Sister swings open the door and leans her seat forward, waiting for me to squeeze behind her into a whole new world. The creamy white car is brilliant under the sun. The gold trim gleams. I am Cinderella and my chariot has finally arrived.

I drop the trash bag, peel off my gloves.

"Hailee!" Disbelief stains Amanda's eyes.

I hop in. Nikki's sister slams the door.

"Hailee!" A mix of anger, worry, and something else

fills Amanda's face. Her arms drop at her sides. I tell her I'll be right back, and I don't worry because she can still change her mind but she doesn't and then the car roars off, leaving Amanda by herself on the side of Culver Street.

"I can't believe I'm doing this!" I shout to Nikki.

"What?"

I holler again, but the wind roars over the convertible and she can't hear me. My hair ripples like flames against the wind. I breathe in the music. My heart pumps the beat. Nikki shoves her sunglasses over her eyes, nods her head to the tune. I bob my head like she's doing; next time, I will have sunglasses. She thrusts out her hand with her pinkie and index finger extended—rock and roll horns—and she is the picture of cool. This is the movie I want to be in, this music playing as the camera zooms in on Nikki and me just as she flashes the horns. We'll laugh, and even though you can't hear us over the guitars, you'll see what a great time we're having. After a second, just long enough for the audience to focus on us, the car will scream away, like it's going so fast, even the camera can't keep up with it.

I learn at stop signs Nikki's sister is Jordan, and the guy driving is Jordan's boyfriend, Kyle. I like it better when we're moving too fast to talk, when I don't have to think about what to say. I like the way we roar through town, making heads turn.

How you like me now? I want to yell. I am fearless.

Nikki holds up her cell phone and snaps a picture of us. The speed of the car matches the energy coursing inside me. None of it is familiar, and all of it is thrilling.

Kyle rips through downtown Palm Hill and way too soon, we're smack-dab back on Culver Street, and I am dropped off beside a frowning Amanda.

My heart beats with the rhythm of a song I don't yet know.

"You shouldn't have done that," Amanda says. Then, "What was it like?"

As I watch the shiny white convertible drive off, my hair in knots and tangles so bad I'll have to tear them out later tonight, all I can think of is, *It was, like, the best seven minutes of my life.*

Chapter 16

. . . .

Amanda said that after I took off with Nikki, she wished she'd come, too. "I was afraid to. That girl in front was smoking and I don't really know them."

I didn't really know them, either, but I couldn't let Amanda in on that. She talked as though Nikki and I were good friends. All I ever said was how Nikki and I met in the bathroom and how helpful she was and funny, too, like in history class, and how Emily and Cynthia couldn't believe that Nikki Simms spoke to me.

Amanda has me right on top of the popularity ladder, but really my fingers are clinging to the bottom rungs. I just let Amanda come to her own conclusions. When I saw myself through Amanda's eyes, I felt important. I didn't want to change that.

Neither Amanda nor I mentioned my little car trip to our parents. That's the kind of thing you don't have to discuss with your best friend—she just knows. Besides, it's not like I murdered someone or stole something. There isn't one single commandment against riding in convertibles. Still, I'm glad she didn't tell my parents because I'd be in big trouble and then we probably wouldn't be stopping by the electronics store after church today.

Holding my thumb to my ear and my pinkie to my mouth, I pretend to talk on my new cell phone in front of my mirror. Emily's phone is green; Nikki's is red; Amanda's is plain old black because it's not a smart phone with a screen, and black is the only color that kind of phone comes in.

I feel sorry for Amanda because I'm also getting a laptop. All she has besides her dad's old phone is a chunky computer that sits on a desk in their formal living room. I can't believe I used to think she was lucky. Poor Amanda.

I do a few more poses in the mirror before getting ready to put on one of my church dresses. Opening the drawer of my *undergarments*, I push aside my first bra because, guess what? I have outgrown it. This is how it happened: Mom took me to the mall for new clothes. I shopped in Aéropostale and Forever 21 and all the good places, and I discovered something I didn't know before—I hate shopping for clothes. You have to look through five hundred tops before you find one that isn't see-through, doesn't hug you so tightly your belly button is a dark oval shadow that everyone can see, or isn't cut so openly, your bra shows.

As I modeled one top, Mom fingered the strap on my left shoulder. She examined the front of my chest. My *bustline*, as she calls it.

"Mom!" I crossed my arms.

"I think you need a bigger cup size." She didn't even whisper.

I slammed the dressing room door shut, pulled off the shirt, wriggled out of the tank, and put my own clothes back on. Mom tried to pull me to the lingerie section, which is right by the water fountain and the bathrooms. Like, what if someone I knew walked by and caught me holding Sweet Things Bra and Panties, Matching Set? I headed for the door instead, but there were three tops and some shorts I liked, so I couldn't storm out like I wanted to. Finally my mom emerged from the aisle, two bras dangling on hangers from her fingers.

I handed her the clothes, then pretended I didn't know her. When we got home, I rushed the bag upstairs like a hot potato before Dad saw it. For all I know, she tells him about these things. *No, she doesn't; no, she doesn't*, I convinced myself.

So I hook up the new bra and put on the matching underwear, then I slip the green summer dress over my head. Green looks good with titian hair. Usually, I go bare-legged to church, matching my flip-flops to my outfit, but today I'm thinking I should wear stockings.

Like Nikki. I poke my head into the hallway and listen. The clanging of dishes means Mom's in the kitchen. I hear Dad downstairs talking to her.

Tiptoeing through the hall, I slip into their room and head for the drawer I know Mom keeps her stockings in. "Reinforced toe," the boxes say. When I pull out the stockings, big seams and double strips of nylon cross over the toes. I don't want my feet to look like old lady toes. I stuff them back in their boxes and shut the drawer when I spy Mom's makeup sitting on top of the dresser. I wonder how I would look with darkened lashes and shiny lips.

Hiding a tube of mascara and some lipstick in my fist, I check for Mom or Dad, then sneak into the hall bathroom. I twist open the mascara. The wand makes a dry sound when I draw it from the tube. Bristles stick out of the tip, but I don't see any mascara on them. Maybe it's like water paint. I add a couple drops of water to the tube and slosh the wand around. Much better. Black, runny drips splat into the sink as I brush the stick through my eyelashes.

Poison! Poison! Eye poison! The ink runs into my eye. It stings like iodine! I'm blind. I run the cold water, splash my face, and see in the reflection that the mascara has left gray water streaks on my cheeks and red cracks in my eyes.

And then, "Hailee! Need your help." Oh, my gosh, why is she always calling me when I'm busy?

"Coming!" I yell back, my voice muffled by the washrag I'm scrubbing with. I'm not taking any chances with the lipstick. Before she can call me again, I've put the makeup back in her room and I'm downstairs.

This is what Sunday mornings smell like: salty sweet bacon sizzling in the pan; scrambled eggs and cheese; the dark brown aroma of coffee.

Libby kicks in her high chair. "Aa-ee!"

"Libby! Hi, Libby! Hi, Libby!" I sing in a high-pitched voice. Babies like that—babies and dogs—but we can't have a dog until Libby gets bigger, so that's why I put *dog* toward the end of my list.

It's been a month since we won the lottery and I've only gotten four Things I Need: bicycle, cell phone (getting today), laptop (getting today), new clothes (though I can't wear them to school because of the uniform rule).

Dad's plate is empty and he's bent over the checkbook. "Hi, honey," he says, lifting his eyes for a moment.

Mom sets down my breakfast. As she pours a glass of orange juice for me, she says, "When you're done, I need you to wipe Libby up and play with her until church."

"But I haven't done my hair yet." A messy bun looks easy but takes time.

"You can take her into your room." Mom clicks off the burners, closes containers, puts things away. "I've got to get ready."

After she's upstairs, I ask Dad, "Could Libby just stay in her high chair?"

Dad shakes his head. "I'm trying to balance the checkbook, and I want to go through the newspaper and see what's on sale."

Hel-lo? Lottery winner—don't need bargain basements anymore.

He moves into the dining room and I sigh as I hear the newspaper rattle.

"Okay, Libby," I say when I hoist her out of her high chair.

Libby's not interested in any of the toys I stick in front of her. Pulling my hair is more fun. I wouldn't have this problem if I were bald. She bounces from picking up a ceramic vase to almost biting the electric cord to pulling on a bookcase. I bet she thinks her name is "NoNoNo" because I say that a *lot* more than I say "Libby."

I drag her new saucer upstairs. The least she can do is sit in it while I fix my hair. Or so you would think. She bellows as soon as I slide her into its colorful seat.

"WaaAAHHH!"

"*¿Cómo te llamas? ¿Cómo te llamas?*"

"Look, Libby, look!" My dogs-and-babies voice.

Dad calls up, "Hailee, can you please do as Mom asked? I'm trying to concentrate."

Libby squirms in the saucer, and when I try to reposition her, I find a brand-new doll under her butt. She stops crying when she sees it, stretches out her arms, but I hold it closer for a better look. I've seen this doll in commercials; I wanted this doll when I was younger. *Too expensive*, I was told.

Libby pulls on the doll's legs.

I never had stuff like this when I was little. I don't care if we won the lottery or not—they're bringing Libby up to be a lady of leisure. Brand-new saucer, store-bought bibs (as in *not* from garage sales), new clothes, and now Happy Hannah Hearts. I clench Happy Hannah with my fist and she squeaks.

"Aanah!" Libby demands.

It's so unfair.

I yank Happy Hannah Hearts away from Libby. Happy Hannah Hearts has to go to sleep now. Happy Hannah can't play. I take the doll to Libby's room and stick her on top of the changing table, turning my back on her happy little heart.

Libby jumps up and down in the saucer when I come back. "Aanah! Aanah!" she chants.

I bend over and brush my hair, ignoring Libby's cries.

"Hailee, I need you to pay attention to her." Mom stands in my doorway.

I'm upside down looking at her through my legs. Mom's mouth is where her eyes should be and her eyebrows are her lips and tracks of watery gray mascara streak her cheeks.

I flip right side up. Without thinking, my hand rubs my own cheek, which causes Mom to say, "I know—my mascara." She shakes her head.

"Maamee! Maa-mee!" Drama Queen Libby raises her hands for Mom. Her little face is red and bubbly with tears and snot.

Mom lifts Libby from the saucer and nestles her against her hip. "What's wrong, little girl? What's the matter, you? You're in here with your big sister and your saucer—no crying, okay, no crying." Libby shudders with a big finishing sniffle. Mom says, "I'll take her. Bring the saucer for me, will you?"

I scoot the saucer behind Mom. As I pass Libby's room, Happy Hannah Hearts glares at me.

Chapter 17

. . . .

Me: Amanda, this is Hailee. I'm texting you
from my new phone! LOL!

I press send. "I just texted Amanda!" I yell to Mom and
Dad in the front seat. We're on the way home from the
store after church. "I wrote, 'Amanda, I'm texting you
from my new phone! LOL!'"

I have to explain to them that LOL means laughing out loud. Then I text Amanda about how I had
to explain LOL to Mom and Dad. I set up contacts
for Emily and Nikki. I've never called Nikki, but
she gave me her phone number that day in the convertible.

"Turn around, Mom!"

Click! I take her picture. I add her to my contacts

and Dad, too, because they also got cell phones today. "Take my picture, Mom."

She stabs the screen with her fingernail.

"Not like that!" I roar. OMG!

My phone tweedles. "Amanda's texting me!" I read it out loud. All my teachers say I project my voice well.

> **Amanda:** Wow, what kind of phone did you get?

I peck out my answer. "I'm going to tell her you guys got phones, too. And that I got a laptop. Hey, it's fixing my typos!" *Send.*

"Libby!" *Click.* Trees passing by. *Click. Click.*

Now my phone makes a different sound. I slide my finger across to answer. "Hello?"

Amanda's voice blasts through the ear dots. "Oh, my gosh! I can't believe you got a phone!"

"And a laptop!"

"You're so lucky!"

"I know!"

Mom turns around. "Hailee, you're yelling."

I nod. Then to Amanda, "Say hi to Libby." I put the phone up to Libby's ear and hear Amanda's voice. Libby tries to grab the phone. I pull it to myself. "Me again!"

"Yelling," Mom says.

"I'll call you back later," I say. "No! I'll text you!"

Me: I love my new phone. Do you have anyone's number I could put into my contacts?

Send.

I text Emily. Hi, Emily, it's Hailee and this is my new
phone! Just got it! LOL! I read the message, then back-
space over LOL, because why would I be laughing out
loud about getting a cell phone? My thumbs hover
over the illuminated keyboard. I press a colon, then a
parenthesis. Now my message reads, Emily, it's Hailee and
this is my new phone! Just got it! :)

I start to send the same text to Nikki, but then I
change stuff because Nikki is different from Amanda
and Emily, so the text I now send looks like this: Nikki,
it's Hailee. New phone. Just got it.

Amanda buzzes in with a text. She's sent me Tanner
Law's number. Huh. She never told me she had his number. Emily sends a text that, when I open it, fills the
screen with exclamation points. A Christmas-morning
feeling washes over me.

I poke my head up to the front seat and hold my cell
phone in front of me. "Which ringtone do you like better?" I ask Mom and Dad. The first one sounds like a
dull flat line. The second is a silver jagged buzzer. The
third one chirps red notes. The fourth one—

"Stop!" Mom laughs. "You're driving me crazy!"

Dad shifts the rearview mirror. "Plus, I don't want
to work Libby up before her nap."

Libby.

At home, Dad unpacks my laptop, but it's useless until the guy comes to hook up the Internet. I don't mind, though; there is so much to do on my phone. The phone asks me if I want to hook up to a network. I see my neighbor's last name and click on it. I have wi-fi! I click a picture of my cheery red maple, which, now that the new leaves are opening, should be called my chartreuse maple. I click Dad outside on a ladder against the garage, tying the bougainvillea to the trellis with special florist string he bought. I click myself in the mirror, then hold the phone away and up, and click another picture of myself. Then I review my photos. My nose slopes down into a bump; my eyes crinkle into slits. I delete both pictures.

I finger-comb my hair so it falls across one eye. Instead of a big fat smile like in the other pictures, I keep my lips together as if I've got a secret and I'm teasing the other person. Pulling my shoulders back, I hold one arm up, aim, and click.

The playback photo reveals a mysterious girl with dark eyes. It's me but it's not me. I love it. Immediately, I text it to Amanda and Emily to use as a contact picture.

By the time I'm called for supper, I've taken more than a hundred pictures, played a bunch of free games, and decided on my ringtones. I carry my phone down and lay it on the table beside my knife.

You could sharpen pencils on Mom's raised eyebrow.

I move the phone over to the island and take my place at the table.

"Can I open a Facebook account?"

"What's that?" Dad asks.

OMG! I would ROFL, but I'd probably get into trouble or hit a table leg. Instead, I stay in my seat and explain Facebook. Dad and Mom exchange I-don't-think-so glances. Before they can say anything, I point out the benefits—Emily's on Facebook, and probably lots of other people—but the word "no" radiates from their faces. "And some of my teachers have Facebook class pages."

Something changes in Mom's expression.

Knowing I've hit on the right tactic, I press on. "I can use it to keep up with assignments and group projects." Silence. I look from one parent to the other. "I wouldn't do anything wrong on it; I'd set my account to private."

Dad says, "How do you know about all this?"

I shrug. I really don't know. It's like you absorb it from the atmosphere.

Sighing, Dad says, "We're willing to give it a try."

"But be careful," Mom says. "We'll be checking your computer." Then a flood of don't do this and don't do that crashes over me. She drowns me in rules and batters me with regulations. The black hole of parental guidance tries to suck me into its vortex, but I hold on to my chair and keep my mouth closed until it's over and finally the words subside, the table stops lurching, and Libby sticks a green bean in her mouth.

I take a deep breath. Mom sits up; Dad cocks his head. They stretch their spines forward, their bodies asking, *What do you have to say about all this?*

I look at both of them and consider my answer. "Pass the potatoes, please."

★   ★   ★

I've been in bed for only an hour and already I've got fifty-seven friends on Facebook. Amanda isn't allowed on Facebook, but Emily is and she becomes my first friend. Nikki Simms's posts are private. I visit other pages and websites but I keep coming back to Nikki's page. Are we friends? She says hi to me. She took me in the car with her. But she hasn't texted me back about my new phone; I don't know if I should bother her on Facebook.

I won't do it. Instead, I play a hangman game. I look at YouTube. I go back to Facebook.

I discover one of my teachers from Palm Middle. Her wall is private, too, but she left her pictures open. I go into an album called "Beach." She wears a one-piece suit like my mom does. OMG—teachers don't wear bathing suits! They probably have rules against that. In another picture, two little kids bury her in the sand and she's smiling even though there's sand in her hair and on her face. Then she's raising her glass in a restaurant and laughing as if she's a regular person and not a teacher.

You'd think she has this whole other life outside of school. I can't wait to show Amanda.

I lurk through some other pages and finally go back to Nikki's. She was the second nice person to me at Magnolia. I tap into her photos. The "Neighborhood" album contains close-ups and strange angles of old buildings and houses. Some of the photos could be ads for jeans or skateboards, they're that good. She must walk around for hours, there are so many pictures.

I click into "Mobile Uploads." The first one is a Magnolia girl, Alexis, I think. I swipe her picture off. Next is Jordan, Jordan and Nikki, Nikki and—ohmygosh— Nikki and me! "Riding around with Hailee," reads the caption. Our hair whips in the wind and our eyes are brilliant. You can tell we're going fast because the only thing in focus is us.

We *are* friends.

I click the request. Then I type in every name I can think of and blast friend requests into cyberspace. Some of the people I hardly know, but I know *of* them and they must know *of* me, because they accept my friend request. I LOL at some of their posts, and I *like* some of their photos. As I read every story and every comment, I can't help but marvel at this new world I am now part of. It's a parallel universe. People are cooler here, and they look better, too. I upload the new mysterious photo of me as my profile picture.

Someone mentions an app that makes people look older. First, I try it on my own photo, but it doesn't work because my face is angled. I laugh at how it makes Libby bald and toothless. I apply it to Mom's photo. It lays equators across her forehead and creases her skin like a pie crust. It scalps her hair. I feel like I did when I forgot to water my African violets for a long time, and the leaves became crackly and brown. I stare at the fake photo of Mom, then press *delete*.

Later, my phone vibrates in my hand. I startle under the covers, not knowing what time it is or how long I've been asleep. The screen casts a pale blue light in the tent of my sheet.

Nikki Simms: Cool.

I scramble upright. Cool. What is cool? My sleepy mental notes can't remember. Then I realize she's replying to my text from today—yesterday, actually. It's 3:05 a.m. and Nikki Simms thinks it's cool I got a phone.

"OMG," my brain texts to me.

My thumbs type a paragraph about shopping for the phone, but before I press *send*, I press *delete* because what I just wrote is boring. Then I write about riding in the car, but that was two days ago and old news. If I talk about history class, I'll sound like a dork.

I rock on my bed in the dark and think.

Think.
Think.
Think.

> **Me:** Nikki, this is my new phone. Just got it.
> **Nikki Simms:** Cool.

I bite the sides of my cheek, something I do only when locked in serious concentration. Finally, I come up with something to say back.

> **Me:** def

It seems just right. It matches her response. I send it, wait for a second, then put my phone on the nightstand. My clock reads 3:31 a.m. It has taken me twenty-seven minutes to type three letters. I hope she likes my reply.

Chapter 18

. . . .

The whole way to school the next morning, I check my messages. Lots of them, but not one from Nikki. I wonder if we are friends or not. Of course, this would be the morning a car accident holds us up. The red lights of an ambulance swirl while I click around on my phone.

I bounce my legs up and down. I bend to the left and then to the right of the headrest in front of me. "Can you go around?" I ask Mom. I've planned to accidentally run into Nikki to see if she got my request and my text.

"Nope, we're stuck." Then her lips move silently in a whispered prayer for the people in the accident.

When we finally pull up to Magnolia, I have just enough time to get to my first class before the tardy bell rings. Emily panics when I hold my phone under the desk to show her my photos.

"Turn it off! Turn it off!" she whispers.

She keeps herself focused on Ms. Reilly, even when I nudge her and try to pass my phone over. I send her a quick e-mail, but she shakes her head and doesn't reply. My phone vibrates. I bend my head and scroll through my News Feed: a girl from Palm Middle is home sick today. She is eating chocolate ice cream and watching TV.

Ms. Reilly calls out my name. I jerk my head up. I click off my phone and slide it under my thigh. Ms. Reilly asks, "Do I have your attention?"

"Yes." I hope she doesn't ask me what she's been saying.

She goes on with the lesson, and I hold my head in a way that looks like I'm listening. I wonder what TV show that girl is watching. My fingers itch to find out.

After class, Emily apologizes for not taking my phone. "I didn't want to get in trouble."

I check my messages as we walk down the hall. Some are Facebook notifications and some are junk mail. None are from Nikki. When I finally see her in history class, I say, "I've been having trouble with my phone. Did you get my message last night?"

"Yeah, you were up late, too," she says.

I don't know what to say next. "Okay, just checking." I want to ask about the friend request, but I don't know how.

"Okay, dude."

"Okay." I stand by her chair until I realize she's waiting for more. "Okay," I say again and shove off to my own desk.

Mrs. Fuller announces a pop quiz. Everyone groans until silenced by Mrs. Fuller's evil glare.

Nikki raises her hand. "Do I have to take the quiz?" she asks. "I was absent a couple of days last week." She folds her hands on her lap, straightens her posture.

Mrs. Fuller turns flat eyes on her. If they were having a no-smiling contest, she'd win. "Miss Simms, this is a pop quiz. Your attendance, or lack of it, is not my problem."

"But I wasn't here. Don't we get the same number of days to catch up? That would mean I have until tomorrow." I can't see Nikki's face, but her voice is extra polite.

Pinched-faced Mrs. Fuller passes out the quizzes. Grabbing a marker, she writes on the dry-erase board, "N. Simms—Quiz Tues." When the papers reach Nikki, she turns to pass them and catches my eye. She mouths "Ha!" and flashes a tiny thumbs-up, and then sits quietly while the rest of us are tested.

★   ★   ★

Emily moves in stop-animation across my laptop. We are video chatting as we work on our assignments. Emily splits the screen to show me what she's done on the year-book so far. The eighth graders are the senior editors and get to make all the decisions about page design and which candid photos to use. Sixth graders are called contributors. Emily is contributing a description of the Book Fair Family Night.

Reading her words, I feel as though I am there, the buttery smell of popcorn pulling me through the crowd. I hear the little kids shriek as they jump in the inflatables. Neon purple and fluorescent green lightsticks dangle from necklaces.

"This is good," I say to her face on my screen. Video chatting is weird because you're looking at the other person and they're looking at you, but neither one of you glances up at the camera, so you never actually make eye contact.

"Really?" She rereads the words, then I watch as whole phrases are sucked into the screen, replaced with new words that pop in one letter at a time. "What about that?" Emily asks. "Does that sound better?"

Both ways sound good to me. My phone chirps—text message.

Nikki Simms: Hey.

"Nikki Simms is texting me." I hold the phone up to the camera.

Emily's eyes widen behind her glasses. "What does she want?"

"I don't know." But I am thrilled.

Me: Hey.

Hardly a second passes and I get another text from her.

Nikki Simms: Can you believe Fuller today? She's a royal pain in the—

"Oh, my gosh!" I blurt. Nikki has spelled the word properly, in all its swearing glory.

Emily pipes up from the other side. "What does it say?" Enlarging the text with my fingers, I turn the display so Emily can read it for herself. She giggles on the last word. Neither of us says the curse out loud, but even reading it silently feels daring. Emily wants to know what happened with Mrs. Fuller, and I tell her about the pop quiz and how Nikki should have been allowed more time.

Emily doesn't agree. "Pop quizzes are different," she says. "That's why they're *pop* quizzes."

"But you can't be quizzed on stuff you weren't even in class for. It's not fair."

The digital version of Emily freezes in a shrug while her voice goes, "What are you going to say back?"

I can't top that swear word, but I want to show Nikki that I'm on her side.

Me: Royal!

Emily is still frozen. I could examine every single pixel on her face and she'd never even know. I jump when my phone sounds off again.

> **Nikki Simms:** Fuller's evil. All I've done since I got home is work on assignments for her class. It's taking sooooo long. Would you send me the quiz questions? I need to get an A, but I don't have time to study because I've also got a paper due in a different class.

The corners of my mouth drop. I hold the phone up to the computer camera.

"She wants you to cheat!" Emily unfreezes. She's moved in so close to read Nikki's text, all that shows is the top of her head. Coils of her hair spring up against the camera.

I pull my phone away and reread the text. I am aware of Emily moving around on her side of the screen, but I'm more aware of Nikki on the other end of the phone, waiting for my answer.

Emily goes, "Tell her you can't." As if it were that simple.

Reviewing my mental notes, I pull up the video of Mrs. Fuller bragging about flying to Rome, and you know that's exactly what she was doing. That's why it was funny when Nikki said, *I believe the Pantheon is to your left.* Whenever Nikki talks to her, Mrs. Fuller wears a sour expression, like she's tasting something she does not like and never will.

"It's only ten questions," I say out loud.

Emily shakes her head.

"She doesn't have time—"

"No!"

"But she's got other homework!"

"I wouldn't do it," Emily says, all judge, jury, and secret witnesslike. Boingy-boing ropes of hair doodle in front of her face.

Nikki Simms: ?

Emily is frozen on my screen again. Her voice cuts up in dashes and dots. None of her words make it through.

Would it hurt to help Nikki? No one would even know.

"If you're still there," I say to frozen Emily, "I have to log off."

I pick up my phone.

Chapter 19

. . . .

I bet you want to know what I did next.

I called Amanda, who's on her first day of spring break. All she did today was nothing, which is always better than going to school. Thanks to Mom and Dad, I don't get a spring break this year. Magnolia had theirs before I started and Palm Middle is just now having theirs. As usual, I get the short end of the stick.

"How about I come over?" Amanda asks. She was so bored today that she cleaned her room for something to do.

I whisk her upstairs as soon as she gets here. She smells like coconuts and sweat. "Did you lay out today?"

She inspects her arms and asks, "Do I look darker?"

Of course she does. My freckles are jealous.

We sit on the floor. Outside the window, my maple catches most of the sun in its spread-out leaves, flickering patterns of sunlight on my rug. Our backs against my bed, I scroll to the texts between Nikki and me and hand my phone to Amanda.

"You shouldn't give her the quiz questions," Amanda says. Even after I describe Nikki's side of it, Amanda doesn't change her mind. "It's cheating."

"But I'm not trying to cheat; I'm trying to help. She's got all that other stuff to do at the same time. Plus, Mrs. Fuller doesn't like her."

Amanda shrugs as if that doesn't matter.

I'm offended on Nikki's behalf. "Mrs. Fuller is a windbag." I tell Amanda about the Pantheon and Mrs. Fuller's sour face every time she talks to Nikki.

Rrring! Amanda startles at the sound of my laptop's alert.

"It's Emily!" I shriek and pull the laptop from the top of my dresser. "Hi, Emily! Amanda's here."

Amanda leans way over and sees herself in the little square that shows you what the camera is seeing. "Oh, my gosh! This is so cool. Is this video chatting?"

Embarrassment melts my face. "Sorry," I say to Emily. "Amanda's not allowed to Skype."

Amanda scrunches her mouth and asks, "What did you tell her that for?" at the same time Emily says, "I can call back if you're busy."

I press *mute*, hold a finger up to Emily, and say to Amanda, "How about I call Emily back?"

"Why?" Amanda asks. Her voice sounds like crossed

arms. "She's *my* neighbor, too. Or do you have some-thing *private* to talk about?"

"No!" Yes! Private *school* stuff. If only Amanda's parents could send her to Magnolia. We could join the same sports, and I'd go over to Amanda's house every day so Matthew could coach us, even though he's never played lacrosse, but I bet he's good at it.

Emily texts in the chat box: I will call back later.

"Look!" Amanda gestures toward the screen. "You're being rude!"

I gasp at Digital Emily and scramble to click the sound back on. "Sorry!" I say for the second time. I guess the three of us are going to talk now, because I can't ask either one of them to leave—someone's feelings would be hurt.

"So," I say, "did you practice your flute?" I'm asking to be polite, but also because I don't know what else to say, since I'm friends with Amanda, and I'm friends with Emily, but I've never been friends with Amanda and Emily.

Amanda leans so close to the laptop, I bet Emily is counting her pores. "Can you play something?" Amanda asks. Gently, I push her back so we can both see the monitor. Amanda peers at the little video of herself and fixes her hair.

Emily's mouth says, "I don't know," but her eyes say, *Yes, yes! Please ask me again.*

I want Amanda to hear how good Emily is. "Play something—something we know!"

We watch as Emily moves away from the screen, pulls out a case, screws her flute together, and returns. I do believe I see a little sparkle behind her glasses. She says, "Do you know Vivaldi?"

"ViBaldy?" Oh, good one!

Amanda elbows me.

"No," Emily says, not getting it. She pronounces the name slowly, in an overly exaggerated manner, her top teeth setting on top of her bottom lip to show me the vee sound. "Vi-*v*aldi," she says.

I move my features into confusion. "Vi*Salty*?"

Emily shakes her head. "Vi—"

Amanda pushes in front of me. "Hailee's trying to be funny. I don't think we know that group."

"Vivaldi was a composer," Emily says, but she says it nicely.

I whisper to Amanda, "A composer, not a band."

"Well, you didn't know either!"

"But *I* didn't say anything!"

A couple of flute notes trill from the laptop. The song is so familiar; it's . . . it's—

"*Star Trek*!" Amanda yells.

I was just about to say that.

Emily's fingers move like centipede legs over the keys, making spaceships zoom through my head. The flute has an actual voice—not Emily's; it's a flute, not a kazoo—clear and pure at times, and wiggly like a singer at others. It's amazing, really. When she's done, she lowers her flute and her eyes.

"Wow," I say. If Emily went on one of those TV talent shows, she'd win.

"You play so well!" Amanda says.

Emily murmurs her thanks and brings the flute to a whisper before her mouth. The silvery sounds of wind and waterfalls cascade from the instrument. I am in a forest, the mist rising, and goldfinches calling from the treetops. It is beautiful.

When she finishes the melody, I clap and Amanda joins me.

"How do you make that little hole with your mouth?" I ask. "Do you whistle into the flute? How long have you been playing?"

Emily unscrews the flute. "Three years."

Amanda and I say all sorts of nice things about Emily's flute playing. Emily angles her head slightly aside and down, as if she can't face the compliments straight on.

Changing the topic, Emily says, "Did you text that one person back?"

"You mean Nikki?" Amanda yells at my monitor, examining her own face from side to side.

Emily pops when she realizes Amanda knows what she's talking about. She goggles from behind her lenses. Emily asks Amanda, "Did she tell you?"

She. *She!* Like I'm outside the circle, which is wrong, because I am the center of it. "Yes, I told her," I say, even though the question wasn't directed at me. "She—"

Amanda butts in. "I don't think she should do it."

"I don't, either," agrees Emily.

They hardly know each other and they're ganging up on me.

"It's just a quiz." I stick up for myself.

"It's cheating!" they say in unison, then they laugh together.

My fingertips fidget on the edges of the touch pad.

For one thing, neither of them is in Fuller's class; they don't see how she acts toward Nikki. Also, and I can hardly blame Emily for this because she's been brainwashed by Magnolia, but Amanda should know how unfair teachers can be. You saw how I was practically expelled from school for helping Amanda out of a crack just so she wouldn't get laughed at. Sometimes you have what happened, and then you have what *really* happened right behind it.

Emily's voice crackles. Her head tilts up. Her eyes are shy but hopeful. "I'm having a sleepover this Friday," she says. "Do you want to come? You can come, too, Amanda." Then she freezes.

I tap the keyboard. "Are you still there?"

"No, I'm not here."

Her voice is so deadpan, I don't get it for a second, but Amanda laughs immediately.

We agree to ask our moms, and even though I can't see her, I know Emily's got that surprised little smile on her face like she did when I first said I would have lunch with her.

"I always thought she was stuck-up," Amanda says after I log off, "but she's actually nice."

"I just thought she was weird, never coming outside or anything." It's true; in all the years I can remember, I've never seen Emily playing outside. From tricycle to bicycle—no Emily. No tag, no chalk drawing, no skating. I wonder why. "But she *is* nice."

"And funny," Amanda adds.

"Yeah," I say. Not to brag or anything, but I'm pretty funny, too. For instance:

Man: The dog ran away.

Lady: Doggone it.

See how quickly I made that joke up? That's how funny I am. Sometimes even your own best friend can take you for granted.

Amanda and I go downstairs, where Mom is folding clothes and Libby is working hard at unfolding them.

Amanda swoops Libby off her feet. "Happy Hannah Hearts!" She picks up the doll and makes it talk to my baby sister. "Hi, Libby!" Then she pushes Hannah into Libby's belly, making her giggle.

Mom watches them and smiles. "Amanda, would you like to babysit this Thursday?"

"Babysit? Sure," she says at the same time I ask where Mom's going.

Mom runs her hand down a towel before folding it in neat little squares. "Just errands. Maybe you could get one practice diaper change in before you girls do something else?" Mom brightens her eyes and aims a smile at us.

I groan, but Amanda hitches Libby on her hip. Well, it's fun to do stuff when it's not your regular chore *and* you're getting paid for it. I never get paid to watch Libby. I make a mental note to add *nanny* to my list of Things I Need because neither Dad nor Mom is going to come up with it.

Amanda's all excited about babysitting when she gets up on her still shiny pink bike and rides home. March flutters by me in windy scarves scented with magnolia. The beads on the crape myrtle rattle to each other, stirred by the breeze. A little chill ripples up my arm as cottony, purple-blue clouds mushroom across the sky. I head in, grab my phone, and rush upstairs.

> **Me:** I forget some of them, but here are the quiz questions I remember.

★   ★   ★

The next morning, I walk straight to Nikki's bathroom. When I push the door open, a girl I've seen before,

Alexis, I think, bounces off the wall and throws something white into the toilet.

I hear a flush, then Nikki emerges from the stall, smiling when she sees it's me.

"She's cool," Nikki tells Alexis.

Alexis doesn't seem so sure of it. She picks up her backpack, says good-bye to Nikki, and walks past me out the door.

I keep my voice casual. "I didn't hear back from you. Did you get my text?"

"Oops! I meant to text you!" And here she touches my arm. "You're a lifesaver!"

I was right! She really needed those quiz answers. I'm so glad I could help.

Nikki goes on. "Fuller will rearrange the questions on the retake, but they'll still be the same ones. My parents said I'd be grounded if I get another C on my report card, and I would die if I got stuck with Mimi." Rolls her eyes.

"Who's Mimi?"

Nikki assumes a haughty face. "Mimi—Miranda Simms—my mother." The thin, tan lady I saw outside Nikki's house my first day at Magnolia. Nikki lifts her backpack to the sink and rummages around. "You want a smoke?"

My face has a heart attack.

Nikki laughs, but not meanly. "Just kidding. You're too young to smoke." She sticks a cigarette into the corner of her mouth, tilting her head. A lighter comes out of nowhere, and when she pulls on the cigarette, I inhale at the same time.

A song plays from inside her backpack. "Mine," she says. She leans her head so the smoke doesn't go into her eyes as she roots around for her phone. Silently, she reads whatever's on the screen, then scrolls and reads other messages. Occasionally, she taps her cigarette into the sink.

I stand by like a dolt. I don't know why I came here. I don't have anything to say and I don't know what to do with myself. In fact, I'm gearing up to make some kind of excuse to leave when she clicks her screen a few times, puts her phone away, and washes her cigarette butt down the drain. She hefts her backpack on and gestures me to the door.

As we walk into the bright, sunny morning, Nikki Simms says, "I just accepted your friendship."

Chapter 20

. . . .

So I'm on my bed later that night checking statuses of all my friends and discover in Nikki's photos the girl who left the bathroom when I came in. Her name *is* Alexis. Almost all the photos of Nikki are pictures other people have taken and tagged her in. I'm looking through them on my laptop when Megan *likes* a photo I posted of Libby. Why would she do that? You can't *like* my sister if you don't *like* me—that's not how it works. I go to her profile, sort through her pictures, and spot one of her and her family hugging Mickey Mouse at the Magic Kingdom. I *like* it. See how she *likes* that!

Pleased with myself, I move on to Tanner Law. Tanner on his skateboard. Tanner catching a fly ball. Tanner and Amanda sitting at lunch. I click on this one, making it larger. I can tell by the angle that Tanner took this one himself. *Me and Mandy,* the caption reads. Mandy? I've never called her that. I narrow suspicious eyes, examine the slit of space between them, and notice that Tanner and *Mandy* are leaning toward each other. Just a little—you might not notice it unless you study it like I'm doing, but there it is.

Keeping that photo up on my laptop, I grab my phone and text Amanda.

> **Me:** I saw a picture of you and Tanner on Facebook.

Her response comes back in seconds.

> **Amanda:** Yeah, we sit at the same table.

I stare at the picture. The space between them is shaped like a triangle. My thumbs create more words.

> **Me:** Does he still like me?

Moments pass. My phone doesn't tweedle with her reply. Electronic minutes are worse than dog years or grown-up time, because when someone is online and doesn't respond right away, time melts you like an ice cube on the sidewalk and your molecules change from one form of matter to another. My molecules change from curious to impatient. I examine the Amanda and Tanner picture on my laptop.

Tweedle!

Amanda: Don't be mad at me, but . . .

"What are you doing still up?"

"Mom!" I slam down the lid of my laptop. "You should knock!"

She gives me the eyebrow and crosses her arms.

"Sorry!" I say immediately. My hand creeps like a daddy longlegs, covering my phone.

Tweedle!

Amanda: I think I like Tanner.

I whip the phone under my covers.

Nothing escapes Mom, not even the red-shouldered hawk. She takes the laptop off my bed and sneaks her hand under my blanket for the phone. Her movements are as crisp as the corners of my sheets. "I'm sorry, too, but you're supposed to be sleeping, not . . ." She shakes the phone in the air.

I rise like a puppet drawn up by strings. "Where're you going with my stuff?"

"I'm keeping it in our room so you can sleep." Her voice walks down the hall with my phone and laptop. "You'll get it back in the morning."

Leaping out of bed, I zing down the hallway after her. "I said I was sorry." No response. "Can I at least text Amanda back? Could I just let her know I have to get off the phone? You don't want me to be rude, do you?"

Mom stops so suddenly, I almost bump into her. Slowly, she turns.

Mom: ☹
Me: ☺

My shadow dives into bed before I do. It's barely midnight. My cheery maple scritches its leaves against each other, throwing sharp patterns of moonlight and shade against my wall. Crickets warble short blasts that sound like my coach's gym whistle. Frogs bleat from the woods. It's weird how they suddenly stop, all at the same time. Then one frog solos a few bars and the rest join in again. A tiny little freeway with froggy drivers, all blaring their horns—that's what they sound like. They don't sound like *ribbit*.

Speaking of which, Amanda and Tanner. I purse my lips. I lie flat on my stomach with one leg hooked up. I try my side, my back, and my other side, but I can't get comfortable. Alexis tagging Nikki. Megan *likes* my photo. Amanda likes Tanner. Why? "Ugh! Science." "Got new shoes—*like* them if you like them." "My new skimboard!" "Chocolate or strawberry?" " 'Dr. Who' is

my new favorite show." All this stuff is happening without me.

I think I like Tanner.

I need my phone.

Chapter 21

. . . .

Emily DeCamp lives in a converted attic. Once you open the door, you have to climb a short flight of stairs, and the space opens up to the best room ever in the world. Pine floors shine their honey gleam, and thick, furry throw rugs—purple and pink—beg your feet to come and bury your toes in them. A white rocking chair with a quilted pillow sits in the corner in front of shelves loaded with books. New item for my list: convert the attic into a super-huge bedroom and call it Hailee's Kingdom.

Amanda's come with me. I wasn't sure if she'd be comfortable, since we're all Magnolia girls and she's a public school girl, but she called Emily back that same night and said she wanted to come. I'm wearing a new denim skirt and a yellow tank with a rainbow-colored peace sign on it. Amanda's outfit, I've seen it before, but

Emily hasn't so I guess it will pass. I just hope nobody looks too closely at Amanda's knit top—it's pilling.

I creak across the floor. Emily DeCamp has the entire Dr. Seuss collection, including *The 500 Hats of Bartholomew Cubbins*, which is so old no one even thinks about it anymore except for me. And Emily DeCamp. I finger classic editions of Nancy Drew, Hardy Boys, and The Baby-sitters Club. Margaret Peterson Haddix fills half a shelf. This is what I call living.

The ceiling slants at odd angles, and dormer windows make hidden cubbies. One of them has a small door. For monsters. Ha-ha, just kidding.

"Your room is so pretty!" Amanda squeals.

"Pipe down!" I order out of the side of my mouth. I glance around like I'm used to this kind of stuff. "Is anyone else coming?"

Emily thrusts her glasses up. "Marna."

"Who's that?" I peer out one of the dormers. Emily has a perfect view of the road and the front yard.

"She plays the oboe."

"The elbow?"

"No, the—"

"Don't mind her!" Amanda says. Her eyes kaleidoscope over the whole room like a tourist at Disney. "I love your room! I always wanted a canopy bed!"

Amanda's acting like a fangirl. It's sort of embarrassing. I'm not saying I don't like Emily's four-poster bed with a neon green canopy and matching daisy bed-spread; I'm just saying you don't have to gush all over it.

Every room in Emily's house has been torn from the pages of Amanda's mom's magazines, from the tongue-in-groove wood floors to the cool tile under our feet in the kitchen. Mrs. DeCamp serves us pizza and root beer. Mr. DeCamp takes pictures. "Smile," he says. *Flash!* You'd think Emily never had friends over before.

When Marna finally gets here, we rush upstairs, and for the first time ever, I hear Emily giggle. "What do you guys want to do first?" she says, shutting the door.

A small media center holds a TV, a DVD player, and a laptop. "Check Facebook!" I say. "Watch a movie! What do you have?" Leaping up, I riffle through her DVDs and spot ten right off the bat I'm dying to see.

"We could do that any old time," Emily says. Of course *she* can—she owns the movies. Some of us aren't that lucky.

Majority votes we play Monopoly. Each one of us gets a fuzzy rug to sit on and I choose the wheelbarrow because I think it's fun to push a real one. I own one property by the time my ringtone goes off. Someone has commented on a Facebook post I've commented on. I check my News Feed to see what else is going on.

"Hailee!"

The iron, the dog, and the top hat are all looking at me. Amanda goes, "Put your phone down, silly. I swear!"

I take my turn, then scroll through different comments on my phone.

"Hailee," Amanda says in a half-scolding, half-serious voice.

"Wait a sec." I finish reading the sentence I'm on. "Yeah?"

She almost pulls off a Mom eyebrow. "It's your turn."

Monopoly is the longest, most boringest game ever invented. Amanda keeps prodding me when it's my turn, and later when we change into our pajamas, she whispers to me, "You can't be texting all the time! It's so rude."

"I wasn't texting," I hiss back. "I was checking Facebook." She has no idea. You have to keep up with it or you'll be behind what everyone else has heard. "You're the only one here who isn't on it."

Since I didn't know who else was coming to the sleepover, I brought my fancy pajama set Mom bought me from Macy's. I tried once to wear it at home, but the lace edges picked at my skin. Marna wears a peasant nightgown, and Emily emerges from the bathroom in a hot-pink tank with print bottoms.

Amanda is so out of place in her old PE shorts and graying T-shirt.

I pretend not to notice, but Amanda's my best friend, so whatever they think of her is going to spread to me. Time for diversionary tactics. I jump on Emily's bed and almost tear the canopy. "Truth or Dare!" I yell.

"No, Light as a Feather, Light as a Feather!" Marna shoots back. "We played it at the last party I went to and the girl actually levitated!"

We are amazed. Somehow it's decided I will be the girl they try to lift. Marna says we need at least four lifters, so Emily goes downstairs and comes back with her mom.

Mrs. DeCamp has toodley-doo hair like Emily's, but she holds hers back with a headband. Perfectly shaped eyebrows frame dark brown eyes, and freckles sprinkle her nose, which is Emily's nose. She sits crisscross next to me. Mom would probably call her Lady DeCamp, but I like sitting by her. She's nice.

"Do you wear contacts?" I ask.

She smiles—a perfect row of white teeth, but not too white like some people who get carried away and practically strip the enamel off theirs. No, hers are natural looking, just like her makeup and her manicured nails.

"How did you know? Are my eyes red?"

"No, no! I figured maybe you did, since Emily wears glasses."

"I just started wearing contacts," she says, talking like she's one of us. My mom is always too busy with Libby to sit with my friends. "But when I was you girls' age, I looked just like Emily, glasses and all."

"Mo-om!" Emily's nose pokes out from her hair.

"It's true." She reaches over and smooths Emily's mop from her face. "Except you're prettier than I was."

"Mom!"

Mrs. DeCamp gently laughs. "You girls are so easy to embarrass! Okay, what are we doing here?"

Marna explains the game. I am to lie still as a statue. Each lifter will stick the first two fingers of each hand under my body: Marna at my head (since she's in charge); Mrs. DeCamp on one side, Emily on the other; and Amanda at my feet.

"Thanks a lot!" Amanda pinches her nose as if my feet actually stink.

"Smell the roses!" I wiggle my toes in her face.

Marna lowers the light and settles us down. "This only works if everyone believes," she intones. "Hailee, you are light as a feather and stiff as a board."

"Light as a feather and stiff as a board," I repeat. Amanda tickles the sole of my left foot. I ignore it. I concentrate all my energy on being light as a feather, stiff as a board. My blood is pine sap that hardens the wood, so now I'm stiff as a board and heavy like one, too. Instead, I try to think feathery stiff thoughts.

"Close your eyes. Everybody, close your eyes. Hailee, you have to be quiet, but everyone else say it with me. Remember, if we believe, we can make her levitate."

Marna starts the chant. "Light as a feather, stiff as a board. Light as a feather, stiff as a board." The others begin. Their voices join as one and fill the room with a hypnotic spell. I open one eye, spy through the slit.

Marna rocks as she chants. Her features knit in concentration. Emily and her mom murmur the words in low voices. When I glance at Amanda, she doesn't sense it. Her head is bent and she's more serious than I've ever seen her. A chill goes straight through me and I squeeze my eyes shut.

"Light as a feather, stiff as a board; light as a feather, stiff as a board." The chant gets louder; their words get faster; and on some signal I can't see, they begin to lift. "Light as a feather, stiff as a board; light as a feather, stiff as a board." Louder, faster, fingers pressing against me. "Light as a feather, stiff as a board; light as a feather, stiff as a board—ohmygosh—it's working!" someone says, which causes all their voices to heighten.

I open my eyes again, watch their mouths flap in unison, and suddenly laughter rips open my gut, breaking the spell.

"Hailee!" Amanda is clearly disappointed.

"It was working," Marna declares.

I burst into gales of laughter. I was the board, and I can tell you right now their fingers were not lifting eighty-seven pounds of Hailee Richardson.

"You should've seen your faces!" I roar. I mimic them, rocking and all. Amanda gives me sourpuss lips. I point at her as I chant.

Mrs. DeCamp laughs and tells us she's got work to do. "Emily, did you remember to take your allergy pill?"

Emily leans her head back against the bed. "Yes, Mom," she says in an oh-my-gosh-you-remind-me-every-day-why-are-you-doing-this-to-me-in-front-of-people voice.

Mothers. They can be so embarrassing sometimes.

Still, this is new information for my mental notes. "You have allergies?"

"Grass, weeds, tree pollen."

I can't believe it. "You mean like, basically, everything outside?"

Amanda pipes up. "That's terrible! I'd feel like a prisoner."

For a second, Emily looks hurt, like she's a strange laboratory rat we're all examining. But then she says, "I'm used to it. Besides, I can go outside a little bit; I just can't stay out or I'll start sneezing, coughing, and my eyes get all scratchy. I mainly need to be in."

We always thought she was weird. It's just allergies! I guess you really don't know a person until you know them.

★   ★   ★

The moon slowly makes its arc from one dormer window to the other and we are snuggly and wide-awake in our sleeping bags. Emily had braces in elementary school and might need them again. Marna actually hates the oboe. She wanted to play drums, but her parents said no way. Amanda talks about Matthew's new girlfriend, Shana, and how she sees the two of them kissing.

When a boy touches your cheek, his fingertips leave glittery paths of sparkles and happiness across your skin and somehow these sparkles bubble up to your brain and you feel as if you are floating. Even though Matthew was swatting a bug off my face, this is what it felt like.

Amanda goes off to a different subject, but unanswered questions pile up in my mental notes: Who starts the kiss, the boy or the girl? Do you have to close your eyes? (I would like to keep mine open, at least the first time so I could see what's going on.) What if the boy has just eaten half a bag of spicy barbecue potato chips? Do you still have to kiss him or can you ask him to go brush his teeth? You see what I mean here. No one ever tells you the rules.

Marna asks me what it feels like to be rich. "I don't know," I answer. It's hard to explain how we won three million dollars but we aren't rich. I mention taxes, investments, and installments, but I can see she doesn't know what those things mean.

Marna says, "I can't believe you could win three million dollars and be poor!"

"We're not poor!" I don't even wear my Goodwill clothes anymore. "It just feels like we should be richer. But I did get some stuff, like this phone and my laptop."

"You got some new outfits," Amanda points out.

"Yeah, new outfits," I say.

"And a new bike," Amanda adds.

"Yeah." I can't believe I forgot the Treads Silver Flash 151.

"And you get to go to Magnolia."

"O-kaaay," I say, drawing out the last syllable. Except for Amanda, everyone else here has the same stuff I do. "It's not like I'm spoiled or anything."

"Maybe not spoiled, but you guys are all so lucky!" Amanda gushes.

"Lucky?" I am indignant. Who pedaled a red boy bike for years and endured the Megan and Drew tag team of insults? Whose mom used to drive a little farther because the Goodwill store near the gated communities had newer clothes on their racks? I'm not lucky; I'm finally getting what I deserve. Seems to me there're two flavors of lucky—the kind that tastes like a chocolate sundae with whipped cream, M&M's, sprinkles, chocolate shavings, hot fudge, and a maraschino cherry, or the kind that tastes like canned peas. I have spent most of my life with a heaping plateful of the second kind.

I don't want to talk about luck and money anymore. Instead, I put Amanda on the hot seat. "Amanda's not allowed on Facebook."

"Really?" says Emily, and from incredulous Marna, "Why not?"

Amanda kicks me from her sleeping bag. In a tight voice, she explains her parents' rules. After tossing that bone, I thought they'd be busy for a while, but it back-fires. They sympathize. Their parents are strict, too. Their parents insist on reading their posts and have controls that block some websites and turn off Internet access at certain times.

"That's horrible! My parents would never do that." To prove it, I slip out my phone and tap on Facebook.

The first thing in my News Feed pops my jaw open.

Tanner Law likes Amanda Burns.

"Tanner likes *you*?" I blurt.

"What?" Amanda springs up. The other girls rustle with curiosity. Amanda leans over, glances at the screen, then takes my phone. Her mouth bows into a little smile.

I'm confused. "Why did he write that?" I don't *like*-like him, but I liked him liking me.

Amanda gets all shy. "I guess he just sort of . . ." Shoulder shrug. "He just—" A smile breaks on her face like the sun popping up in the morning. "He put a note in my backpack, but I didn't see it until I got home. He said he likes me and . . ."

"And what?" Emily asks breathlessly.

"Just stuff." She lowers her gaze, stares at Tanner's post. Her eyes reflect his words, are full of *Tanner Law likes Amanda Burns*. "He wants me to write him back."

"Why?" I hate how my voice sounds—big and demanding—but still I want to know.

Amanda hears it, too. I realize this because she makes her voice small and sweet. "He wants to know if I like him."

You'd think she just announced a new Harry Potter book. Emily and Marna clamor to see his photo and then pronounce him "cute" and "hot." Emily likes his curls. Well, of course she would.

Watching them, I invent a new word—*boyzonbrain*. Sounds like a poisonous berry, doesn't it? It means boys-on-the-brain and it's even more dangerous. I make a mental note to submit my new word later.

Emily asks Amanda, "Are you going to write back to Tanner?"

"What're you going to say?" Marna chimes in.

"Could I have my phone back, please?" I'm irritated Amanda's kept this from me, and I'm annoyed that Emily and Marna act as if Tanner's post is worldwide news. Here I was, concerned for poor Amanda and her ugly clothes, and there she is, taking over the whole sleepover.

"One minute," Marna says. She, Emily, and Amanda rate the pictures, comparing Tanner to different singers and celebrities.

"Oh, yeah, I forgot to tell you," I say like it's not even a big deal, "I sent Nikki those quiz answers." The only girl who responds is Amanda, who glances up just long enough to shake her head at me, then goes back to looking at Tanner's face on *my* phone.

When something simmers in a pan too long, it doesn't boil over or burst into flames—it quietly bubbles until it's charred and black. My charred black heart becomes tough as an overdone pork chop. In the dark room, all I can see are their smiling faces illuminated by the glow of Tanner's photos.

"I need my phone back," I repeat. "I have to check my messages."

I read through my News Feed, gasping or chuckling here and there so Emily, Marna, and Amanda can hear how interesting my friends and I are.

In fact, the comments and posts I read come through as a loud noisy room, a party where it's all happening. I'm right in the middle of it when snippets of Amanda's conversation penetrate my bubble. She's asking what CSS means; she raves about the new dresser she got as a hand-me-down from her aunt; she talks about riding the city bus. My cheeks burn with shame. Though Marna thinks it would be exciting to go on a bus, she says, "My mom would never let me do that."

Of course she wouldn't. Only poor people do that. I cringe at what Emily and Marna must think of Amanda—must think of *us*. Right away I say, "Well, *I* don't ride the bus." It's true. I don't take the city bus, but that's because Mom and Dad haven't renewed my pass in over a year. Nevertheless, I want to separate myself from the picture Amanda has created.

Mom picks us up the next morning after Mrs.

DeCamp has filled our stomachs with thick, sweet slices of buttery French toast. I'm relieved to get Amanda away from my Magnolia friends. She has nothing in common with them.

As we ride home, I whip out my phone.

"You were on that thing all night and at breakfast, too," Amanda says. "It was kind of rude."

What can you expect from someone who shares a clunky computer with her parents and isn't allowed on social networks? I ignore her. Mom aims her rearview mirror to talk to me. "You *are* on that phone too much, Hailee. Put it away."

The look I give Amanda is dirtier than the soles of my feet on a summer day.

On Sunday, I don't go to her house to help her choose outfits. Maybe Tanner should help her. Maybe she could hop on the bus and get advice from a department store lady. Maybe the flea market is holding on to a faded, pilling top that is a perfect fit for her.

I am so glad I don't go to Palm Middle.

Chapter 22

. . . .

Nikki: Ditching school. Meet behind electric shed at south gate.

It's Thursday morning, and not even the surprise fire drill Tuesday made my heart flip out as it does now. Mom smiles and waves as she pulls away; after lunch, Amanda will babysit Libby while Mom runs errands. Since the weekend, I've been careful to keep Amanda separate from my new friends; I don't want them to think of me as hobo Hailee. When Mom's van turns the corner, I read Nikki's e-mail again.

Nikki's sent a group message that includes me, Alexis, and another girl named Gia. Skipping school. Nikki's skipping school and she wants me to come.

Alexis: On my way! Hang out by Lake Eola?

Lake Eola! My heart drops. I love the swans and the ducks and the way they flock over for bread crumbs. In my backpack is a sandwich waiting to be torn apart and fed to them. For a second, I am under the cypress trees laughing with Nikki. The Lake Eola Fountain shimmers in the sunlight, birds are chirping, and there's a rainbow even though it hasn't rained.

Without looking up, I avoid other girls streaming onto campus as I stare into my phone like it's a crystal ball.

> **Gia:** Dude! My mom almost read that! Be right there.

I frown. The next adventure of my life is starting without me.

If I go, Nikki and I will probably be best friends. If I don't go, I'll look like a dork and Nikki won't like me. She'll drop me from Facebook and not say "Hey" to me anymore. Why do I have to be a good citizen? Why? Why? Why?

The bell rings. I grit my teeth.

> **Me:** I am a loser and a dork. Have fun without me.

I don't really write that, but I might as well have because Nikki will realize it sooner or later. My feet shuffle down the path, finding the way to my first class while my mind dashes for the perfect words and phrases. My life at Magnolia hinges on what I say next.

Me: Cool.

Okay, good start.

Me: Cool. I might have a test today. Say hi to the swans for me.

When I press *send*, I feel like I've just lost something that I won't be able to get back.

★   ★   ★

This day is intolerable. The digital clock on our class monitors couldn't move any slower. It's like dog years times adult years, especially as I sit through the class Nikki's supposed to be in. I am the only one with a heartbeat as everyone else moves in slow motion. No one cares about the cavernous black hole that is Nikki's desk, but my eyes are drawn to it like paper clips to a magnet.

They're at Lake Eola. I'm the doofus at school. Honor roll, Library Club, perfect attendance, could I be any dorkier? Mom's to blame—she raised me to be this way. *Education is important. Be a good citizen. Honor thy father and thy mother.* God needs to make a commandment for parents: *Give thy kids a break.* I suffer through history and my last class and only then do I feel a bit of relief because I spot Alexis back on campus to catch her bus home.

Their day at Lake Eola being over, my day of torture ends as well. All my suffering has worn me out, and I trudge like a mule with a heavy load to Library Club.

"Still tired?" Emily asks, referring to the excuse I gave her at lunch when I sat like the hunchback of Notre Dame and glowered at my milk carton.

I throw my backpack behind the return desk. I need to talk with someone about this. Clicking over to my messages, I hand my phone to her so she can read the entire order of events. One library cart is full of books ready to be reshelved. Tugging it out, I say, "I'll be right back."

Dewey Decimal is a blanket on top of all your other thoughts. No matter what's bothering you, Dewey will take your mind off it. As I work my way down the stacks, I talk to myself inside my head. *Arc, Arc—Archer comes before Architect.* Sliding the books into the proper places gives me a sense of satisfaction. You can't help but feel that way when everything is in order.

When I tote the cart back, Emily is checking someone out. Mrs. Weston leans over the return desk looking at something. Squinting her eyes to focus on a phone left on the counter. *My* phone. I rush the cart closer. The display is lit up. The gray frame of my e-mail program is open.

Oh, my gosh. Oh, my gosh.

I whip the cart around the desk on two wheels and scarf up my phone. "Hi, Mrs. Weston."

Her eyebrows knit in the middle, a point of concern. "Hailee, I just saw something on your phone that was not good."

Emily blanches behind Mrs. Weston. Her eyes bug out. "It's my fault. I put the phone down when I had to check out the books."

"I'm surprised with you girls." She quotes from our handbook the oaths to report cheating, drug use, and other non–Magnolia behavior. "Hailee, may I please see your phone?"

I slide my fingertips across the screen, accidentally deleting the string of incriminating e-mails; at least it feels accidental when I do it. I'm horrified and relieved when the e-mails slurp into the little trash can. When I hand the phone over, my inbox is full of noncriminal activity.

"What happened? Did you just delete that message?" She flits up and down over my inbox.

I tremble like a Chihuahua. "I don't know! I don't know what I did!" And I don't. I mean, I know what I did, but I don't know how I did it—I had no out-loud thoughts of doing it.

Mrs. Weston says, "Girls, I'm going to have to report this to the office."

"No!" I step closer to her. Suddenly I know the

exact meanings of "implore" and "beseech." "Please don't. It's my fault."

She waits for me to go on, so I do.

"I left my phone out. It's not Emily's fault or anyone else's. My phone should've been in my backpack. If I hadn't shown it to Emily, she wouldn't have put it down and you wouldn't have read it." I'm throwing everything out there. "Plus, aren't those private? I'm sorry, but aren't e-mail messages private?" My lungs pump air fast. My hands feel clammy.

Mrs. Weston's face is full of reproach. "Hailee, I'm disappointed with you. Just saying you're sorry doesn't excuse what you've done. A true apology means owning up to the actions you're responsible for." She rolls her head back as if seeking advice from above.

I hope he throws some down for me, too. I'm in a world of trouble, which would be okay if it were just me, but this is a chewed-up gum ball rolling in the grass picking up everything in its path. "Emily didn't know anything. I only now showed her."

Sighing, Mrs. Weston glances back at Emily. Emily's nose and part of one eye show through sprigs of frightened hair. "Emily, please go to the second floor and straighten up the nonfiction."

Emily mouths "Sorry" when Mrs. Weston isn't looking.

"Exactly what did that e-mail say?"

I can't believe I'm being interrogated. She can stick

me in a reading room, put the spotlight on me, and feed me only bread and water. I won't be the pigeon. I won't sing. Nobody's going to call me a snitch. Besides, she wants to know *exactly* what the e-mails said. God is my witness and so are you—I don't remember the *exact* words.

I shudder with a million sighs. "I don't know," I say honestly.

Mrs. Weston lets out her own cool breath. "Hailee, I'm a pretty fair judge of character. I know you're a good girl, a conscientious student. Were you aware that you're supposed to report things like this?" She gestures with the phone before handing it back to me.

I shake my head. Mom read the manual on student conduct, not me.

She nods her head. A decision has been made.

"Are you going to call my parents?" Tears wet my eyes.

Taking a moment to consider my question, Mrs. Weston speaks with a softer voice. "I don't believe I need to. You know right from wrong." She crouches and snags books out of the drop box. "And *you* didn't skip."

Relief floods my body.

"But I'm going to have to report what I read."

Volts of electricity slam from the top of my hair to the tips of my toes. My mind flashes with a bright light, a bright blank light. I am zombified.

My brain is a sluggish battery starting a car. A plan I

can't read yet forms in the back of my mind. My body obeys, strapping on my backpack, smoothing down my hair. I hear myself telling Mrs. Weston I just remembered my mom is picking me up early. I'm aware of Emily bending over the rail, her loopy masses hanging in spirals.

My feet know where they're going even if the back of my head hasn't told the front. I text Mom and tell her we're doing something special in Library Club today and that I'll text her when she has to pick me up. Mom doesn't like to text. *Takes too long*, she says, so the phone rings, and it's her telling me to have fun and be careful and all that kind of mom stuff.

I've seen these streets and houses flying by from the van windows, but everything is different on foot. For one thing: it's hotter. My toes itch with sweat from Magnolia socks and shoes. My backpack feels like a turtle hanging on. I unbutton the very top button of my shirt and tug at the already moist collar.

The roots of old grandpa oaks turn up the plates of the sidewalk. I walk through the peaks and valleys. Lizards scurry away from my feet. The April sun is doing its best to make this the most miserable walk I've ever taken. Cars pass me, bumping down the brick road. The last of the azaleas stretch their pale pink flowers through white picket fences like an offering. They brush me gently as I pass, but I can't stop for them because I'm on a mission.

The yellow house with white columns is even

bigger when you're standing on the sidewalk in front of it. The circular driveway is long enough to hold three or four limos, maybe five, but right now, not a single car is parked in it. Live oaks grace the side yard with their old and twisting branches, forming a leafy canopy and deep dark shade. Italian cypresses, erect as nutcracker soldiers, flank the huge wooden double front doors. Flower boxes hang from the second-story windows, spilling over with every color in the crayon box.

This is Nikki Simms's house.

I take measured steps across the drive, working up my courage, wondering what I'll say, how she'll react. Sweeping, polished steps take me to the door before I'm ready. Bracts of bougainvillea drape from a trellis in a large clay pot. The vines are tight, controlled, close-clipped. I wish Dad could see them. When I lean in to inspect, one of the vines pinches the pad of my thumb. I snatch my hand away, suck on the pain.

Raising my uninjured hand, I make a fist and rap on the door. The wood is so thick, I'm not sure my knock has made it through to the other side. I should leave right now. If Nikki gets in trouble, she wouldn't know I had anything to do with it. Why didn't I think this through? My heart beats double-time. I've got to get out of here, get back to the library. If I hurry, Emily will still be there, and I can slide in next to her and pretend none of this happened.

Relieved, I pirouette on the steps.

Then I hear locks being turned, a creak, and a whoosh.

"Hailee Richardson," Nikki says. "What are you doing here?"

Chapter 23

. . . .

Nikki leans against the front doorway. A gust of cold air-conditioned air rolls out from the inside. Behind me are the empty driveway and street. Nikki asks, "Did you walk here?"

I swallow and nod. My skin steams inside my sweaty Magnolia blouse. I wore the shorts today, but since they go down to the tops of my knees, and the socks come up to the bottoms of my knees, it's not like the outfit lets you cool off.

A voice shouts from inside. "Shut the door!"

Nikki lowers her eyelids in response. "Come on," she says and swings the door more open for me.

Usually, I have to ask before I go to a new person's house, but there's no way I'm going to be a Goody Two-shoes with Nikki waiting on me. Besides, I've always wondered what it would be like inside this place.

The tiled foyer holds a baby grand piano. I wonder if anyone plays it.

"Who's here?" Jordan's voice scrapes against the high ceilings from another room. "You're not supposed to let any of your little friends in."

"Shut up," Nikki responds.

I follow her over tile floors so pretty they put my mom's countertops to shame. Statues of women—one naked!—stand in arched niches throughout the hallway that takes us to the kitchen.

"Oh, my gosh!" I can't help it. "My mom would love this kitchen!"

Jordan's dark head whips around from the couch in the family room. "I *said* you're not allowed to have anyone over."

I freeze. My last footstep echoes.

Jordan's words have no effect on Nikki. "Just watch your dumb vampire show, okay?"

Behind Jordan, pale teenagers live their lives on a huge flat-screen TV. A stone fireplace takes up another side, and the third wall is floor-to-ceiling windows overlooking gardens with cobblestone paths leading you deeper and deeper into the shade. *This* is how I thought *we* would live after winning the lottery.

Jordan puffs on a cigarette and gazes at me. "Chain gang."

"Her name's Hailee." Nikki pulls a frosty mug out

of the freezer, fills it with lemonade, and hands it to me. "Let's sit on the veranda."

"No company in the house while Mom's gone."

Nikki shoots her a look as we cut by the couch.

Jordan groans with irritation and whirls back into position in front of the vampires. She seems to forget us as she puts the cigarette to her lips and inhales.

Nikki flips her off.

My eyeballs sproing out of my head. I steal a glance at Jordan, who has seen nothing except really white-skinned girls brooding.

The veranda is a screened patio bigger than my living room and dining room put together. The patio furniture is set to overlook the gardens, and a stone path on the opposite side leads to a pool. Nikki motions for me to sit on a glider with her and I obey, glancing around to take it all in. The veranda is like the Garden of Eden. Braided ficus trees show off their teardrop leaves. Plumbago rambles over its pots, tumbling in soft blue cascades. A fountain murmurs with water so prettily, I could lie on this glider and listen to it all day and be happy.

"I love your house." In the movie of my life, this will be my home.

Nikki taps out a cigarette from a pack lying on the wrought-iron cocktail table. Lighting it, she invites me to have one by holding hers out.

I shake my head.

She grins, takes a drag. "Sorry, I keep forgetting. So what's up?"

Holding my lemonade with both hands, I take three big gulps before I can speak. Then I tell her about showing the e-mails to Emily and how Emily had to check out books and that's when Mrs. Weston saw my phone and read the messages.

Shadows cross Nikki's face, like when vultures or fast-moving clouds block out the sun, and the earth flickers from light to darkness, causing squirrels and rabbits to hide from what could be a bald eagle plunging from the sky to break their necks and carry them off. Even a red-shouldered hawk can't fend off an eagle.

When I'm done, Nikki blows a thick stream of smoke straight into my face. I'm scared to turn away. I don't want to look afraid, but wispy fingers of smoke scratch my throat, and I gulp down more lemonade to stifle my urge to cough.

Her ice-blue eyes pierce me as she fires off questions. "Why did you show Emily my e-mail? What else have you told her? Did you know she would tell Mrs. Weston?"

I reach out but stop short of touching her. "No! I didn't know she would tell! I mean, she didn't really tell—she left the phone out, but I don't think she did it on purpose."

"Emily DeCamp."

"Yes." But when Nikki relaxes with satisfaction, I say, "I mean, no! It wasn't her fault."

Nikki cocks her head. "So it's your fault."

"No, no . . . it's not my fault, either. It—it—"

"It's somebody's fault. Maybe it *is* your fault. Maybe you did it on purpose because you were mad we left without you."

"That's not why! I did wish I'd gone with you, but I wasn't *mad* at you. After you guys left, I felt like—I felt like—" And then I say a four-letter word that even my parents don't use.

I say it for Nikki.

A part of me feels guilty for swearing, but I stuff that part into a closet I'd just discovered in my heart. Words are just sounds, right, and I offered up that word because I knew she'd understand exactly what I meant by giving it to her.

Nikki's pupils constrict. She scans me like one of those X-ray machines at the airport. I'm as still as a rabbit and ready to be flayed. Scan complete, Nikki whumps against the back of the glider and we move. Only, if you've ever sat on a glider before you know it doesn't sway up and down like a swing; it moves back and forth, back and forth. Nikki speeds it up by pushing against the terrazzo floor.

Leaning into her cigarette, she takes a long, slow drag and releases it to the side. She turns on her lopsided grin. "So you wished you'd come?"

Her words form a life preserver and I grab on to it. Nodding, I say, "I kept thinking about how much fun you guys were having and how I was stuck in school."

"You didn't really have a test, did you." See how I used a period there instead of a question mark—that's because she didn't *ask* me if I had a test; she was telling me she knew I didn't. It was a statement, a declaration, something I could not deny.

I lower my head. My voice is tiny and my words are small. "I was afraid to say no."

I feel her hunch closer. "Are you afraid of me?" she asks.

My throat closes up. I'm afraid of her the same way I'm afraid of tall roller coasters and upside-down rides. I'm afraid the ride will be too fast and too high and even though someone who works there sits at the top of the first hill, you can't really get off once you get on. And yet, if I walk by the ride enough times and hear the people screaming and watch them smile and shake their heads when they unload—*That was awesome!*—I know if I leave without riding that ride, that'll be the sorriest day of my life.

"No." My voice comes out garbled. I clear my throat and repeat, "No, I'm not afraid."

I lift my eyes and meet hers. My stomach feels sick. I put my foot down and stop the glider.

Nikki gives it one more push, watches my face, then stops. "Mimi isn't going to be happy tonight. But it wasn't your fault." She crosses her arms. "It was Emily's."

Before I can protest, Jordan slides the door open and snatches the cigarette pack from the table. "Buy your own," she snaps. "Get the roast in."

Nikki straightens her posture. "You're supposed to take care of that."

"I'm busy. Do it or I'll tell Mom."

The two sisters stare at each other, a battle of the wills, wills so stubborn, there's no telling who might win or how long it could take.

Finally, Nikki blinks and says, "Whatever," which Jordan takes as victory and flounces back into the house. Carefully, Nikki presses the lit end of the cigarette into the ashtray, putting it out. "I hate sisters. Do you have one?"

A video of Libby pops up. Libby laughing with me over the Cheerios on her tray. Libby kicking her legs for joy because I've come into the kitchen. Libby and her fuzzy baby hair. Libby throwing tantrums. It reminds me of *Beezus and Ramona*—Libby is sometimes a pain like Ramona, but mostly, I love her.

I set my lemonade on the table. "Want to trade?" I ask, not because I'd ever want to, but because saying it makes me sound cool.

It works. Nikki gives a reluctant laugh, a laugh that says, *We're in the same boat*, and I try to look like someone who might really be in the same boat as Nikki Simms.

As I hurry back to school before it gets too late, I whip out my phone and post on Nikki's Facebook wall.

Me: Dude, thanks for the lemonade.

She's not mad at me. She's not mad at me at all. Something bothers me, itching my mind like a no-see-um, those bugs that are so tiny you can't even see them; the only way you know they're on you is because you feel them biting, which doesn't hurt like a dog bite or a bunch of piranhas, but it makes you scratch your shoulder and then your knee and you look for a mosquito but you don't see one. That's how you know it's a no-see-um. It's one of the few words that means exactly what it says.

So that's how I'm feeling as I walk back to school, like being bothered by a no-see-um, or in this case, a no-remember-um—when you *know* there's something you forgot but when you search your brain, it's nowhere to be found and then you think maybe you didn't forget anything at all, maybe you just drank too much root beer or something. You ever get that feeling? It buzzes through my head halfway back to Magnolia. Only halfway though, because then I realize that bothersome feeling is probably left over from the way I felt on my way *to* Nikki's house. Now I'm coming *from* Nikki's house and it's okay. She's not mad at me.

I scratch my arms. Stupid no-see-ums. They bite your skin, suck your blood, and fly into your ears straight to your brain. I take off running all the way back to school.

Chapter 24

. . . .

Later, zooming through my neighborhood on the Silver Flash, I ponder about Mrs. Weston telling our principal, and how Nikki's mom will act if she gets a phone call. Probably whack the heads off some broccoli. I'm on my way to fill in Amanda to see what she thinks, and I want to tell her about going into Nikki's house. She is going to be so impressed!

I zip past the other houses, past the orange trees, which are done blooming. They're done with oranges and done with flowers. Time to concentrate on growing. I smile when I hear the hummingbird notes of Emily's flute as I pass her house.

When I get to Amanda's, I bang on the door. My knock is as distinctive as a ringtone. As I wait, I check out the unfamiliar skateboard resting nearby. My pulse quickens. Maybe Matthew bought a new board. I study it so I can make a casual comment about it, like, *Cool board. What kind of wheels are those?* Or—and this is even better—*Can you ollie?* I heard that word on a stunt show and filed it in my mental notes under M, for Matthew.

I'm daydreaming about how impressed Matthew will be with me knowing the word "ollie" that I startle when Amanda opens the door.

"Hey, Amanda," I say and barrel in, almost bumping straight into Tanner Law. "Oh!"

"Hi, Hailee." Tanner Law has shot up a foot since I last saw him. Blond hair glints off his arms, and his eyes, which I've never noticed before, are gray.

Amanda looks bashful. "We were just hanging out."

Then I go all the way into the kitchen and see Matthew and Shana sitting, their fingers entwined on top of the table.

Awkward moments are *so* awkward.

"Hailee! We haven't seen you in a while." Mrs. Burns ducks from the fridge with a bottled water.

I rush to her side. "Well, you know, I've been busy at school and with homework and the Library Club"—I sneak a peek at Amanda and Tanner—*Amanda and Tanner!*—"and have you been looking at any decorating magazines lately, because I've been thinking about redoing my room"—that's true; I said it before, remember?—"and maybe you have some good ideas. My favorite color is green." I can't seem to remember why I rode my bike over here.

Mrs. Burns sips her water.

"Your favorite colors are pink and purple," Amanda says.

"I just changed it." I cross my arms, drop them, and recross them. "People do change, you know."

Amanda gives me a quizzical look.

"Actually, I might have a couple of new magazines." Mrs. Burns starts toward the hallway.

"Oh," Shana says, "would you please finish your story about Matthew first?" Her face and Matthew's face blush in unison.

Remember that game "Which one of these things doesn't belong?" I am living it right now.

As we take seats around the table, Mrs. Burns says, "Hailee didn't hear the first part, so I'll catch her up." I shrink at my name. I don't want anyone singling me out—get it?—because I am already singled out. Anyway, Mrs. Burns picks up the story. "When Matthew was in about third grade or so, he'd come home and cry about this bully who wouldn't leave him alone at recess."

Shana murmurs a soft "Aww," and she and Matthew exchange a glance.

"I tried talking to the teacher, but this kid just wouldn't stop. Finally, one night, Matthew was not himself at the supper table, so Mr. Burns laid down his fork and knife, wiped his mouth, and said, 'Matthew, the next time he bothers you, kick him in the shin.'"

All around the table, we burst into laughter.

"I didn't like the idea," Mrs. Burns said, "but after supper, Mr. Burns showed Matthew where the shin was and told him the only way to do it was to kick hard, then run!" She starts cracking up. "So the next day, Matthew comes home happy, saying he did just what his dad told him to do, and we were glad because we thought that was the end of it.

"But it wasn't. Matthew liked the idea so much that he started looking for that kid just so he could kick him in the shins." Now we're all laughing. Matthew looks embarrassed, but pleased, too. "We had to order him to stop. But that boy never did bother Matthew after that!"

"I shut him down," Matthew says, a sheepish grin lighting up his face.

"Well," Mrs. Burns says to me. "Let me go get those magazines."

Shana says she has to go and Matthew walks her out. I'm alone with Amanda and Tanner. Little hearts float up from their side of the table. Girlfriend and boyfriend vibes soak the air like humidity. When Mrs. Burns comes back, I can barely focus on her talk of color palettes and themed bedding. Matthew slips in and up the stairs.

I don't hear Tanner's joke, but I laugh when Amanda starts laughing.

She looks at me appreciatively. "It's so true, right?"

"I know," I say, letting my laughter die down in a way that sounds natural.

Tanner's chair is about three inches from Amanda's. They don't seem shy except for when they look at me.

"So how's Magnolia?" he asks.

"Oh, it's great!" Amanda answers for me. "Hailee's getting all As and everyone there likes her."

I shrug. "Well, I don't know if *every*one likes me. . . ."

"Of course they do, silly!" Amanda says.

"Yeah, you have lots of friends on Facebook," Tanner adds.

Mrs. Burns puts down her magazine. "Your mom lets you on Facebook?"

Amanda pokes her mom with a glance. "I *told* you, Mom! Tanner and Hailee are friends on Facebook."

Mrs. Burns tilts her head. "But they already *are* friends—in real life."

"Mo-om." Amanda uses a singsong voice. "You're so last century."

Mrs. Burns stands and bops Amanda's head with her rolled-up magazine. The table feels unbalanced after she leaves. I can hear the electronic hum of the refrigerator, the air-conditioning, and the love connection between Amanda and Tanner. I clear my throat. Tanner chuckles at nothing, and Amanda smiles. Her gaze ping-pongs from me to Tanner and back again, and I realize how odd three is as a number.

"Um—" Wet concrete pours into my veins and stiffens my joints. "I have to go home," I say.

Amanda makes sure the door shuts behind her when

she walks me out. "What do you think of him? You can be honest."

She wants me to say something nice about Tanner.

I tilt my head like Nikki does. "I can see how you like him."

"I know! Isn't he cute? He's going to help me with my last project for the Compass Club—cleaning cages and giving baths to the animals at the shelter. He's so awesome!" She bangs her hands together as if the Tanner Law awesomeness is too much to behold. Lowering her voice, she says, "If he tries to kiss me, I'm going to let him!" Her eyes widen with the shock of what she's just said.

So do mine.

I leave Amanda's house without getting to use "ollie" in a sentence with Matthew.

My tires spin off sand on her driveway. Amanda and Tanner or maybe even Matthew could be watching me from a window, so I put a half smile on my face as if I'm thinking about something pleasant, such as lemon meringue pie. (If you aren't a lemon meringue person, think of a pie you do like, such as blueberry or pumpkin.) I sit up straight on my bike and, as I pedal, I point my toes because models always do that.

It's not a natural way to ride, so I'm glad when I'm out of eyeshot and they can't stare at me anymore. I slump over my handlebars and heave the bike side to side while pumping.

Ever since I left Palm Middle, Amanda's been keeping two lives: her regular life (her family and me), and her Palm Middle life (Tanner). I decide I am insulted—*insulted!*—by Tanner replacing me on Amanda's Compass Club project. Out of the generosity of my heart, I offered to help Amanda even though I was really busy, what with winning the lottery and all. I click up to a higher speed. Yes, that's what I'm feeling—insulted.

Furthermore, this whole thing with Tanner. Was she going to tell me? I mean, I only found out through Facebook, and even my stopping over today was unplanned. The thought of her keeping secrets grates against our friendship same as my bike chain grates against its axle. *Big deal*, I tell myself—I keep secrets from her. Things she has no idea of, like how dingy some of her shirts look and how dumb she sounds when she asks things like *What's CSS?* when everyone at Magnolia knows it stands for cascading style sheets. Emily and Marna were polite enough to not point out anything, but at the sleepover, Amanda acted like Little Orphan Annie seeing Daddy Warbucks's mansion for the first time.

I'm plodding by Emily's house when I spy her sitting on her porch steps.

"Coming home from somewhere." She states the obvious as I roll up her sidewalk, careful not to crush even one blade of their perfect grass. Today must be Annoy Hailee Day.

"Yep." I set up my bike, then drop beside her. "I

heard you playing your flute before. I felt like sitting on your porch and listening to it."

Her surprised little smile makes an appearance. "Do it."

"What?"

"Sit on the porch. My mom won't care."

"That would really be okay?"

"Yeah, and then leave me a signal that you were here, like . . ." She glances around. She snaps off a twig from the bushes, breaks it in half, and lays the halves as an X behind the banister. "This will be our code."

I love this idea. It makes up for all the weirdness at Amanda's house and I almost feel normal as I fly home.

Almost normal, but for that nagging no-see-um feeling.

Chapter 25

· · · · · · · · · · · · · · · · ·

"MOM!" I scream from my bed the next morning. It's after nine o'clock—I'm going to be tardy. I *can't* be tardy! How could she let this happen? "MOM!"

"MOM!" I scramble down the stairs. "MOM!"

She bounces Libby on her lap, sitting at the table with Dad. Dad's home. Dad's home?

"Mom, I'm LATE!"

Why are they calm? What's wrong with them? I grab one of the bakery doughnuts off the counter, shove it in my mouth, and circle the table chopping the air.

Mom says. "Relax! No school today."

"It's FRIDAY!" I wave my non-doughnut arm around. "Not SATURDAY!" Rivers of blood surge through my veins.

"We're spending the weekend at Daytona Beach." Mom smiles at Dad.

My heart thunders. I sprint laps in the kitchen.

"Honey . . ." Mom laughs.

I quicken my pace. "It's not funny. I'm going to get in trouble. I can't skip school."

Dad says, "We're all playing hooky today."

My hands fist in alarm. My arms bend, ready to punch if they weren't frozen in place.

Mom smirks at Dad. "Ryan, don't do that to her! Daddy and I were talking about how you didn't get a spring break this year. And between winning the lottery and you changing schools and everything else, we decided the whole family could use a break. I've already called the attendance office."

So I *am* skipping school!

I hug Mom. I hug Dad. I hug Libby even though she didn't have anything to do with it. "Day-ton-a! Day-ton-a!" I make sharp movements with an imaginary baton as I march in front of the sink. "When are we leaving?" I yell like a cheer.

"As soon as you're ready," Mom returns.

Quick as a cricket, I'm up the stairs. My teeth are brushed and so is my hair. I throw everything I need into my pillowcase and hammer downstairs. "Ready!" I sing.

Wait till I post this!

Tap, tap. Tap, tap, click. Oh, no. *Tap, tap.* My phone is dead. "My phone!"

Dad takes it, clicks around, and gives it back. "You can charge it at the hotel."

Groaning, I roll my head back. "That's a long time from now."

"Hailee—Daytona Beach," Mom says. "You should be happy."

"I am! I just wanted to tell everyone else. Oh! Let me go get my laptop."

Dad stops me. "You don't need a computer on our vacation, Hailee. It's time to hit the road. There's a beach out there calling my name."

There won't be anyone calling *me*. My battery is dead, dead, dead.

Libby is so lucky. She falls asleep almost instantly in her car seat. Without my phone, the trip is long and boring. But I must admit, when the van climbs the high bridge over the Intracoastal Waterway, I start getting excited. A pelican perches on the wall with his back to us. He's waiting for just the right fish to come along, then he'll dive-bomb into the water for lunch. Though we're still a few blocks from the sand, I can see a red prop plane flying over the beach with a banner trailing behind it. Dad rolls down the windows and the salty sea breeze rushes through.

A strange, wonderful feeling gets me when we reach A1A. It's the end of the road, literally. When I gaze through the front windshield, there is no horizon. No bridges, no crossroads, no buildings. The blue sky meets the blue ocean and it's a profound sight, seeing eternity right here on earth.

After we're checked in, Mom and Dad want to settle our stuff. The room is big. It has a kitchen! And a separate bedroom for Mom, Dad, and Libby. I get to sleep on the pull-out sleeper sofa. But I can't dillydally on that—the view from our balcony causes my stomach to drop. We are directly on the ocean.

I grab my mom's arm. My words are lost because I'm so happy.

Eleven stories high. A flock of seagulls stretches out their wings and coasts the air current right past us. The wind and the water roar in my ears. The waves whitecap, then crash on the shore in perfect rhythm. I taste the salt with every breath I take. I smell the fishy seawater. Laughter and music from the pool below sparkle in the air. Yellow, red, and blue beach umbrellas decorate the shore, and kids run into the waves followed by adults. My eyes water for the beauty of it.

Mom kisses the top of my head. "I'd better go help Dad wrangle Libby into her bathing suit." But she lingers for a moment as if she can't tear herself away from the balcony, either.

There is so much to take in and I want to remember it all. When I gaze out as far as I can, the line of the ocean is round. I am seeing the curve of the earth—the actual curve of the earth. This ocean was here before me and will be here after me.

The lull of the waves and the foreverness of the sea make me feel like the ocean is a spirit, old and wise, and I'm going to stick my feet right into it.

*   *   *

Libby's face contorts as she curls her toes in the wet, squishy sand trying to walk normally, but even her best effort makes her look like a man walking on the moon. Mom holds her hand, chuckling. The waves mute regular conversation—laughter and seagulls are the only sounds that pierce through.

Before we left our room, I plugged in my phone. Not only do I want to check my messages, I want to take pictures.

Dad stands beside me at our umbrella. "Let's go," he says, and I run in front of him into the waves. The ice-cold ocean shocks me, but I know I'll get used to it. I sputter salt water. "A little farther," Dad urges. "I'll teach you how to bodysurf."

He tells me to hold on to his neck as he swims deeper and deeper. A force of water picks up height and speed. "Dad!" I yell. I don't think he hears me. The water rises into a high wall. I'm scared. I'm scared—oh, God! And it slams down on us. Water, salt, and sand rush over my head and drag at my legs.

But my dad is a porpoise. He kicks his legs and we jump out of the surf, me riding his back like a trainer on Shamu. When we're up for air, Dad's face is energized. "That was great!"

I'm trembling. I'm in over my head, but I've got Dad to hold on to and that's all I need. He explains to me what waves to watch out for and which are the best, and when a good one comes, he launches me like a rocket.

I'm doing it! I don't know how, but I'm doing it! I bodysurf so close to shore that when I stand up, the water is barely more than knee-deep.

We bodysurf, we splash in the shallows, and we all build the best sand castle probably ever made on Daytona Beach. Later, we stroll the boardwalk. T-shirts, beach towels, flip-flops—anything you want, they've got it. We stop for ice cream cones and keep walking. I lick and twist mine around, not letting one single chocolaty drop fall to the ground.

The Daytona Beach pier is boarded up and shuttered down for remodeling. Cables run on posts over it, but the chairs for the sky lift have been taken down. The restaurant, the trinket shacks, even the fishing end you have to pay to walk on are all closed. I feel kind of sad seeing it in this state.

But the colorful Ferris wheel rising on the other side picks up my spirits. A Tilt-a-Whirl spins nearby, and other rides light with excitement. "Come on!" I start for the Ferris wheel because there's a line and I want to beat anyone else going for it.

Mom yells, "Wait!"

I quickly turn around and, oh, my gosh—Libby has picked this exact moment to start fussing. Selfish, selfish, selfish. Libby's tired, Mom and Dad say. They are, too, they say. As we head to our hotel room, I glance backward at the giant wheel and its huge gondolas. I can't wait till we come back tonight.

In our suite, the first thing I do is grab my phone and good thing, too, because I've got a million messages.

> **Nikki Simms:** Dude, I mean it. Text me back. Urgent!

About an hour ago. Urgent! She must be in the hospital. My phone's full up with texts from her. Mom's opened the sliding door to the oceanfront, but I can't concentrate with all that noise. I shut it hard.

Dropping onto the couch, I start at the bottom of Nikki's texts and scroll up. It's like reading a book backward.

> **Nikki Simms:** Text me back.
> **Nikki Simms:** I'm not kidding. Your friend Emily sucks.
> **Nikki Simms:** Urgent! Text me back.

A vice clenches around my chest. The time stamps on her texts show she's been trying to reach me since this morning.

Nikki Simms: ?
Nikki Simms: ?
Nikki Simms: ?
Nikki Simms: Where are you?
Nikki Simms: I'm in second period. Meet me in the courtyard at lunch.

Dad wanders in. "Take your shower. We're going out to eat and then we'll ride the Ferris wheel. Sound good?"

I hear him. I lay my eyes on him, but I can't pop out of the bubble I'm in with Nikki. "Just a minute, okay? I need to text someone."

"No," he says. "Give me your phone."

I panic. "Why?"

Irritation flickers across his face. "I want you to take your shower. Plus, it wouldn't hurt for you to be off the phone for a few minutes. I'm starting to think the only way your mom and I can talk with you is if *we* text you."

All through my shower and all through blow-drying my hair, the only thing I can think about are Nikki's texts. Did Emily go to the principal about Nikki skipping? Did Nikki punch Emily out? I need my phone back.

When he gives it to me in the elevator going down, there are no bars.

"Hailee," Mom says.

The doors have opened to the first floor. Finally, some reception. I follow the backs of my parents as I stare at the screen, which is taking forever and a day to load. We step out into the night. The ocean, the people—all form a busy backdrop to my trying to tap out a text to Nikki.

"Hailee!" Dad calls sharply from a distance.

Somehow, I've fallen behind strangers. I jog past them and catch up to my own family.

Dad's somewhere between anger and worry. Mom shakes her head.

Me: Nikki, are you there? I'm at Daytona Beach.

Dad holds out his hand. "Phone."

Wrapping it with both hands, I hold it close to my body. "Please, Dad." I'm utterly begging. "I just need to see something."

His eyebrows drop. As we weave through the crowd, I stare at my phone, tapping when it dims. I need to be right there when Nikki replies. Dad holds Libby on one side and Mom's hand on the other. I hold on to my phone, willing it to bleat with Nikki's reply.

Arcades and rides light up the night, and happy shrieks fill the air. Smells of french fries, popcorn, and cotton candy drift down the boardwalk. I am a drone, dully aware of my surroundings while focused on the small point of contact I hold in my hands. My body folds on to a picnic table with Mom and Libby as Dad goes to the concession stand to get our food.

Mom starts. "I wish you'd—"

Nikki Simms: What are you doing in Daytona?

"Turn that phone off." Mom's voice is gray with displeasure.

"No! I've been waiting all day for this text."

Libby starts squalling, pulling Mom's attention from me to her. I'll have to thank Libby later.

I ignore Nikki's question because I know that's not the urgent thing here.

Me: I got your texts.

Dad sets hamburgers and nachos on the table with drinks. I grab a soda and pull the nachos closer. The cheese is just the right kind of melty, stretching into a cheese string before snapping when I grab a chip from the basket.

Nikki Simms: That stupid Emily girl got me into all kinds of trouble. Novey called my parents last night and they had a hissy fit.

Me: What happened?

Nikki Simms: I had to sit there while they took turns yelling at me. My mom said if she has to, she'll call the school every hour to make sure I'm there. My dad put KidTracker on my phone. Do you know what that is? It's a freaking GPS system that tells him where I am.

I don't know what to say. I send her a frowny face, but it hardly covers the situation.

Nikki Simms: Then we had a little "visit" with Novey this morning. They talked about my grades, my absences, and my "attitude." Your little—

Dad grabs my phone, slips it into his pocket. "This is ridiculous. You spend more time on that thing than you do with real people."

My jaw goes slack. "But, Dad—"

He stops me with his hand.

"Mom," I plead. No use.

"I'm staging an intervention," Dad says. He's trying to joke, but this isn't funny. I ask in a super polite way for the phone back. I wheedle and whine and use puppy-dog eyes, but Mom and Dad are firm—they'll give the phone back in the morning. For now, they say, enjoy the beach with us.

I'm as shuttered down as the dark Daytona Beach pier.

★　　★　　★

The sun is a yellow scoop of sherbet rising over the morning waves. I wake up with it. Below, towels lay out on lounge chairs around the pool, saving places for people who probably went back to bed after sticking their towels out there.

A family swims in the pool, but the water for the twirly slide isn't on yet. Going down would be a butt scraper. Plus, I'd be afraid of a security guard coming out if I even tried. Joggers, just a few of them, lope across the beach, but it's otherwise more or less empty.

I turn from the windows and sigh.

Do I dare get my phone from Mom and Dad's room? Libby won't wake up, and Dad—he's snoring like a bear. His low, deep snorting and gurgling rumbles through the walls and into the living room. If Mom can sleep through that, she can sleep through anything.

Padding up to their door, I roll my feet, cracking any bone that needs it because I sure don't want anything cracking in their room. Grabbing the door handle, I turn it s–l–o–w–l–y, then creep in. My phone sits on Dad's nightstand.

I tiptoe around the bed, trying hard not to giggle at Dad's thunderous rumbles, then pick up my phone.

Nikki Simms: Then we had a little "visit" with Novey this morning. They talked about my grades, my absences, and my "attitude." Your little friend Emily has a big mouth.

No, she doesn't! She didn't even say anything.

The rest of Nikki's texts are more of the same, each one more bitterly blaming Emily, calling her words I would never use, and cursing her own parents.

I have no idea how to respond. Just then, Dad snorts, startling himself and waking up Mom, who narrows her eyes at me. I'm standing right there with the phone in my hand.

Mom is fully awake, pointing her hands and jerking her head as she lectures me about obedience and manners. Libby wakes up and thinks *Everyone's here!* and shouts her Libby Language while prancing around in the crib. I begin to argue with Mom, and the room fills with a mishmash of accusations and interruptions until Dad slams his hands down on the bed and says, "Enough! Gimme that." Never have I seen Dad's mouth so angry. "I'm sick of this phone. You obviously can't discipline yourself with it, so I will—you're grounded from your phone for two weeks."

My face morphs with horror. I open my mouth but he cuts me off.

"And your laptop is just for schoolwork."

I stew on the couch while they stir in the room. Bathing suits are snapped on, breakfast is made, lotion is applied. Mom and Dad are in good moods, holding hands and laughing at Libby and her moonwalk on the sand.

Nobody but me notices that the castle walls we erected yesterday have been eroded by the tides and all that's left is a shapeless glob of wet sand.

Chapter 26

. . . .

I am miserable with my own company and my sunburnt shoulders when we get home Sunday night. Daytona Beach gave Dad and Libby caramel-colored skin. Mom is as white as ever, having spent most of her time under the umbrella or SPF 70 sunblock. If she had climbed to the roof of the hotel, moonlight would've reflected off her and guided ships and boats to safety.

Before I go to bed, Mom rubs aloe vera onto my back, soothing the burn I feel on the outside but not the botheration roiling on the inside. (And if you don't think botheration is a real word, go ahead and look it up.) My pajamas sandpaper against my skin and I'm in a foul mood when I wake up for school Monday morning. Did Nikki send me more texts? Did Emily practice her flute? Did that one girl whose name I can't remember study for the algebra test she was so worried about?

I don't know the answer to any of these questions because I'm grounded from my phone.

When I swish into my seat first period, Emily smiles her little smile. Well, sure, of course she would. Everything is normal for her; her phone didn't bubble over with molten trouble this weekend. She's so lucky. I sprinted across campus clutching my backpack as if it were a blankie or a shield, but Emily DeCamp is walking around without a care in this world.

"Do you even know what happened after you showed Mrs. Weston my phone last week?" I blurt, interrupting her good mood talk about writing photo captions for the yearbook.

For once, her hair isn't blocking her face, but something seems to shut down around her and divide us. She says, "I didn't show her your phone—that was an accident. You know; you were there."

"Whatever." A slice of hurt cuts through Emily's gaze, but I dismiss it. "Nikki got in big trouble and it wouldn't have happened if Mrs. Weston didn't see my e-mail."

"It wouldn't have happened if Nikki hadn't skipped."

"It's not like she hurt anyone or committed a crime."

"Truancy is a crime, punishable by juvenile court." Emily speaks like a brainwashed citizen.

"Juvie! If you knew that, why did you leave my messages open? Why didn't you give my phone back? I had the rottenest weekend and now I'm grounded from my phone for *two weeks* and I'm only allowed to do schoolwork on my laptop."

"Girls." Ms. Reilly appears between us. I'd been so focused on getting across the seriousness of what happened to Nikki, I didn't notice what was happening right around me. "I'm teaching. You're talking. Since I'm not going to stop, you're going to have to. Jacob?" She waggles her fingers at him. "Trade places with Hailee."

Stunned, I don't move.

Ms. Reilly raps my desk. "Now."

Emily and I sit in separate hemispheres.

At lunch, Emily focuses on her food. Cyndi sits next to her. Yeah, that's right—I called her Cyndi. Emily does a pretty good job of pretending I'm invisible. I think she's mad at me for being mad at her. I gobble down my peanut butter and marshmallow sandwich and tell them I have to go; I can't think of a good excuse, so I just hurry up, get out of there, and go to the library. *Cloudy with a Chance of Meatballs* describes my mood exactly.

People all the time browse through the books, pull one out, then decide they're not interested in it. You'd think they'd put the book back where they got it, right? I mean, the empty space is right there like a missing baby tooth. But no, they just stick the book anywhere, or they leave it sitting, unfiled. It's a good thing I stopped by.

I'm putting books into their *proper* places when Nikki meanders into the library, spots me, and makes a beeline for my location.

"I've been looking for you all day," she says.

Usually, people wait until *after* school to beat other people up.

"Did you get my texts?" she asks. Before I can answer, she melts like butter onto a seat. "Did you read my last one?" I shake my head. She goes, "I asked you to delete all the texts I sent you about Emily. I don't want anyone else reading them, okay?"

The stress of the whole weekend drains from me like dirty bathwater. My bones go as soft as the taffy I saw being pulled in a storefront on Daytona Beach. Nikki Simms is still talking to me and she wants to forget the whole thing. If Dad hadn't taken away my phone, I would've read Nikki's last message. I would've been able to enjoy Daytona Beach.

Relief pulls out a chair for me, and I drop into it beside Nikki. "You wouldn't believe what my dad did," I say and then tell her the whole story of him staging a cell-phone intervention and grounding me from the phone and my laptop (because being able to do schoolwork on it doesn't count as being able to actually use it).

"So Emily got us both in trouble. That sucks." Blue eyes glitter under narrowed lids. "That really sucks.

Anyway, forget about her. Alexis and I were talking about having a sleepover, but she can't do it at her house because her parents are going out, and I can't do it at my house because Jordan's having friends over, so I thought we could do it at your house. Do you want to?"

Does the library have books? Is the ocean salty? Does Mickey Mouse have two big ears? "Yes!" I say. Then I think of Nikki's white pillared house with its marble floors and whispering garden fountain. My house is a shack compared to hers. Shame and embarrassment tumble out of my mouth. "My house isn't very nice." I feel disloyal, but it's true. "We need new furniture—some of it's kind of old." Because it's from garage sales. "My mom hasn't really had time to decorate because of Libby." Blame it on Libby.

"Don't worry about it," Nikki says. She means it. "Will your mom say yes?"

I adopt her cool demeanor. "Definitely."

"Excellent." She eyes the nearby bookcase that houses Staff Selections. Her eyes flick to the display; then she reaches over and touches *The Outsiders*—my pick. "Cool. I've read this book."

Sleepover and *The Outsiders*—can this day get any better? I don't think so. I wish I could post about this on Facebook.

Later, when I see Nikki in history class, she says hi

first. As I wade through the desks to my seat, it dawns on me that other girls pull their feet in as I pass. They've been doing that in other classes, too, and in the hallway. One girl picks up her messenger bag and glances at me like a dog wanting to be petted.

Rainbows radiate in the classroom and I swear I hear angels sing. I have reached the inner circle. I am a sidekick—*Nikki's* sidekick. That means I get some of the benefits of being popular, like people moving for me, smiling at me, and probably even talking about me, like, *Hey, you should read* The Outsiders—*Hailee Richardson picked it out.*

Remember when I said this day couldn't get any better? Boy, I was wrong!

After she calls roll, Mrs. Fuller talks about the upcoming field trip to St. Augustine. I try to concentrate, but my mind races with sleepover anticipation. Mrs. Fuller tells us to write down what she's saying because paper and pencil never forget.

Good point. Clicking my mechanical pencil, I start my notes.

SLEEPOVER!

<u>Food:</u> Root beer, potato chips, popcorn, nachos, chocolate ice cream. For breakfast, doughnuts.
<u>Games:</u> Light as a Feather, scavenger hunt, penny pitch, Bloody Mary.
<u>Movies:</u>

Mom and Dad only let me watch PG movies. Too embarrassing. I cross out movies. I'm not sure about the games, either, but I leave them for now.

★   ★   ★

Mom and Dad say yes to the sleepover and all the stuff on my list. I thought they'd say no way, but Dad said it's about time I started hanging around with people instead of my phone.

The school week drags along with a ball and chain attached to each day. Emily has civics instead of history, so she doesn't get to go on the field trip. I don't mention the sleepover to her, which makes me feel bad because I had a good time at hers, but Emily wouldn't mix well with Nikki or Alexis. Especially not now.

Neither would Amanda. Nikki is smooth and cool like an outlaw, and Amanda's completing good deeds for the Compass Club. It's kind of embarrassing.

Tuesday afternoon, Amanda calls on the house phone. I take it into my room and sit on the floor. She asks, "What's wrong with your cell?"

"Nothing," I say, then explain the hard, long story of my chastisement.

"Oh." She's probably pouting on my behalf. "Well, you *are* kind of always on your phone."

What? She's supposed to be on my side. "Amanda, you don't have a smart phone and you're not on Facebook. If you were, you'd understand."

"Well, I don't need a smart phone to understand when someone's being rude."

"Neither do I, Miss I-Can't-Take-My-Eyes-Off-Tanner-Law. Were you even going to tell me he was your boyfriend?" I cross my arms. She can't see me, but I send indignant waves through the phone line.

"It just happened! I swear, that was the first time he'd been to my house."

"What about Compass Club? *I* was supposed to help you with that."

"Like you helped me before? You abandoned me." Icicles hang from each of her words. "Tanner *wants* to help. He's not going to take off just because someone pulls up in a convertible."

Well! "You said you wished you'd come!" I'm like an elephant—I remember everything.

"That doesn't matter. You dumped me!"

"I was gone only a few minutes!"

"You would've done whatever Nikki asked, just like giving her the quiz answers. She's got you wrapped around her finger."

My mouth opens in silent protest. "That's not true. You don't like her because she's cool and pretty."

Pause.

Amanda says, "You know what? You think you're all that now. You act like you're so important with your phone and your Facebook. No one cares that you won the lottery; no one even talks about it anymore. You're just the same old Hailee—or, no, no—I *wish* you were the same old Hailee because then you wouldn't be so stuck-up."

"Well, just so you know, I don't care what happens at Palm Middle. I love Magnolia. And I'm glad I'm not the old Hailee because the old Hailee would care about what you just said and I don't."

I go on. "Oh, and guess what? I'm having a sleepover and you're not invited because *you're not a Magnolia girl.*"

"*I* wouldn't come anyway."

Then I say the meanest thing I can think of. "You're just a witch with a B."

Air rushes over the earpiece as Amanda gasps on her end. All my steam escapes, and I shrink against my bed.

"Amanda?" My voice is tiny.

My ear is still pressed against the handset when I hear the click, then the dial tone.

I am disconnected.

Chapter 27

. . . .

I feel heavy as a rock and stiff as a board alone in my own backyard after the call with Amanda. I pace over our scribble-scrabble grass, then lean against my maple. The trunk rises tall and straight and explodes all the way up in green pointy leaves.

I ramble around in the garage. It's hard to remember what I used to do before we won the lottery. The old boy bike is keeping company with the garbage cans. I shove the trash aside and pull the bike through. The thin rubber tires flub over the ground. Neglect has let the air out. It pangs my heart to see this hardworking bike in such condition. Furthermore, no one should've put it with the garbage without asking me. It's *my* bike.

Sticky cobwebs trail from its handlebars like streamers. I grab one of Dad's shop rags and brush the debris from the bike. I straighten the front wheel. I pump the tires so they go from floppy as an old man's gut to fat as fresh-baked doughnuts. The seat fits my butt like it's been saving my place.

My new bike will understand.

I rasp down the driveway and around the neighborhood in the direction opposite of Emily's, which is also opposite of Amanda's. Little kids shriek and play in a front-yard sprinkler while their mom weeds. A calico cat watches me go by, only his eyes moving. An old man shuffles down the sidewalk, waves, and smiles. He waves and smiles three more times because that's how many laps I do around the block before I turn back to my own garage.

Up in my room, I flop onto my bed and cover my eyes with my arm.

★   ★   ★

"Getting excited for your party?" Mom asks Friday when she picks me up from school. She smiles into the rearview mirror. She likes the idea of me having a bunch of Magnolia friends.

"Yeah," I say. It's the best I can do. I mean, I *am* excited about my party, but whenever I get too happy about it, thoughts of Amanda pinprick my brain. She hasn't answered my calls. At first, it bothered me; then I checked my mental notes and decided she said some pretty mean things herself.

So I showed her.

I stopped calling.

As Mom and I unload the groceries, I picture Nikki, Alexis, and me eating them. Laughing at the TV with popcorn. Whispering secrets in hot-chocolate breaths. Giggling over breakfast in the morning because we stayed up all night long.

When the doorbell rings after supper, I race from the kitchen to be the one who answers the door. "Hi, Nikki!" I bark. If I had a tail, it would be wagging. I grab her sleeping bag, then my eyes fall on her mother. She's beautiful. I know I'm staring, but I can't stop myself.

Mom comes up behind me, introduces herself, and shakes Mrs. Simms's hand.

"Please, just call me Mimi," Mrs. Simms tells Mom. Somehow, I'd imagined her voice would sound as thin and tight as a wire hanger, but it's sunny, like those tennis outfits she wears. She does that chitchat thing grown-ups do, and though I can tell Mom is a little nervous, she does okay.

Nikki Simms is in my house!

"Let's go upstairs," I say, but before we turn around, Nikki's mother makes a throat-clearing sound. So here it is. I ready myself to see the dragon lady in action.

"C'mere," Mrs. Simms says, gesturing with her hand.

Nikki lowers her head. She trudges toward her mom as if being dragged by heavy chains. Mrs. Simms gives her a quick hug, then says, "Have a good time!" She chucks Nikki under the chin. "Don't stay up too late."

"We will!" I say and she laughs, which makes me feel good. When the door closes, I wonder what I missed— Nikki makes her mom sound evil, but Mrs. Simms is nice.

We've just gotten up the stairs when the doorbell rings with Alexis's arrival. I shout like Nikki does and we run down the stairs, but secretly, I was hoping to have Nikki to myself for a while.

After we put Alexis's stuff up, we hang around the house. Neither of them have baby sisters, so they play with Libby like Libby plays with Hannah, and it's all fun and games until Libby's diaper lets out a powerful stink.

Alexis recoils. "That's disgusting!"

"She's just a baby," I shoot back. Everyone poops.

Alexis makes a gagging motion, moves to the other side of the living room, and flounces onto the couch. Thinking this is a game, Libby starts to toddle her way.

"No!" Alexis draws her legs up. "Oh, my God. Please take her away."

Nikki laughs. "Hey, you wore a diaper once."

I cast a grateful glance to Nikki. Swooping up Libby and her squishy diaper, I whisk her into the kitchen, where Mom and Dad are drinking coffee and talking. "Please, Mom, could you change her? I have to get back to my party."

Mom stretches her arms out and holds up Libby. "Uh-oh! Uh-oh! Someone needs a diaper change!" she says playfully. "It's past your bedtime anyway."

Problem solved.

I'm still grounded from my phone and Dad took the laptop out of my room. "Removing temptation," he said as he carried it out. With Libby the entertainer gone, Alexis is quickly bored. She whips out her phone. Nikki checks a few things on hers, too. My sleepover is falling apart. I think of the games I listed—Light as a Feather, Bloody Mary, Penny Pitch—what was I thinking? Nikki and Alexis are too old, too cool for those kinds of games.

I've got it! "What about ding-dong ditch?"

Nikki cracks a grin. Alexis drops her shoulders and stares at me dead-on. "I haven't played that since I was . . . a little sixth grader."

Oh, yeah. Like I really believe she said that by accident. The only reason I invited her was because Nikki invited her.

Nikki stands up. She coaxes Alexis. "It'll be fun. C'mon, it's dark outside and no one will see us anyway."

I'm mortified as I realize I have to ask permission to go outside since it's dark. "I'll be right back," I say. Dad's not in the kitchen, so I go upstairs. Libby's asleep in her crib and Mom and Dad are reading books on their bed.

"Can we go for a walk around the neighborhood?" Technically, not a lie.

Mom lays her book down. "It's late."

"Just around the block. Please? Dad?"

Dad sighs. He glances at the clock. "It *is* late." He

reads Mom's expression, then my desperate face. "Can it hurt?" he asks Mom. "It's almost summer."

Mom stares at him like she can't believe he's disagreeing with her orders. She shakes her head, raises her book, and mumbles something about discipline and structure.

"Go ahead," Dad says with a wink. "One time around the block and come right back, okay?"

I shirk the guilt that tries to cover me and run downstairs, thrilled with my temporary freedom. Nikki and Alexis aren't in the living room where I left them; they're in the kitchen. A liter of soda is out on the counter along with a carton of eggs.

"Change of plans," Nikki says.

"We're eating?" I ask.

Alexis sneers. She opens the carton and counts. "Nine left." Her thin lips move like worms as she smiles. "We're egging."

I gasp, which gives her a sharp laugh. She cocks her head and asks, "Where does Emily DeCamp live?"

Chapter 28

· · · · · · · · · · · · · ·

Nikki and Alexis crush the perfect green Emily DeCamp grass under their feet as we hide behind her mother's van. The porch is a still life of wicker furniture. Emily's window, the window from which the notes of her flute drop like soft petals, is dark with sleep.

I stare at the house where I was light as a feather and stiff as a board and laughing all night. "I don't think we should do this," I say. We could change our minds right now. We could turn around, jog back to my house, and stick the eggs in the fridge where they belong.

Alexis turns slit eyes on me. "Nikki doesn't think it was your fault she got in trouble. But *I'd* be mad at you if I were her."

"Shut up," Nikki says. Her eyes radiate with daring and excitement.

She slips to the corner of the van and motions for us

to come over. Laying down the carton, she lifts the lid. The ammo is ready.

Alexis bends for an egg, but Nikki stops her.

"Hailee throws the first one," Nikki says.

My heart beats in my throat. Blood whooshes to my feet, and a nervous, shaky feeling flows in its place. Nikki holds out a smooth white egg. I search her face for some way out, but her eyes spark like fireworks.

"Emily got us both in trouble. Come on," she says. She bobs the egg in front of me. "Eggs are good for you."

Alexis swipes two eggs and pitches them at the house. The night air cracks with egg yolks. My stomach drops but Nikki and Alexis laugh, grab more eggs, and hurl them. Nikki wraps my hand around one, but keeps up her own attack. A light comes on in the back—Mrs. DeCamp.

"Hurry!" Alexis urges. Her arm is an egg-throwing machine gun.

Nikki sees me standing, not throwing. She grabs my arm and launches it like a catapult. My egg arcs high in the air. It spins like a football and shatters against Emily's window.

"Run!" Alexis jackrabbits down the street.

My leaden feet don't move. My shameful eyes stay on Emily's window.

Nikki shoves me into action. We sprint down the street. I rocket past her, leap over a split-rail fence, and dart through shadows all the way to my own back porch.

All three of us gasp for breath, Alexis laughing between gasps and Nikki saying, "That was great!"

Their eyes are wide and bright under the porch light; energy beams from their bodies like sound waves. They're jazzed, pumped-up, happy. Alexis keeps breaking up as she describes the egg throwing.

Tonight, I'll pray for rain to wash Emily's house so the DeCamps will never know what happened. Tomorrow, I'll put one of my own dollars in Mom's purse for the eggs. On Monday, I will be extra nice to Emily. If I do all that, it will erase tonight.

Alexis is still laughing.

"We have to go in now," I say. I open the back door and hold it.

"Got any more eggs?" Alexis cackles as she passes through.

I close the door behind Nikki and myself. We head upstairs, and I let Mom and Dad know we're back. I'm quick about it, because the guilty feeling I have is so strong, it's like another person standing behind me, ready to pop out.

I pad into Libby's room and peer into her crib. Her sleeping face is innocent. She breathes easily. Her pajamas are white and decorated with green and pink outlines of elephants.

I wish I could stay in here all night.

Chapter 29

. . . .

"Did you enjoy your party?" Mom asks Saturday after Nikki and Alexis have left. We stand by the front door, having just seen them off. "Nikki's mother is very pretty. . . . She's different from how I thought she'd be."

I wait to hear the end of that.

Since I don't say anything, Mom goes, "She just seemed down-to-earth, that's all. I liked her."

I'm glad Mom thought nice things about Mrs. Simms, and I know she wants to hear all about how fantastic she thinks the sleepover probably was, but I can't even remember the good parts to tell her. Instead, I say I'm sick and stay in for the rest of the weekend. My fingers want so badly to dial Amanda's number and whisper the whole story to her, but I know she doesn't want a phone call from me. Probably she would think it serves me right to feel the way I do, heavy with a stomach full of rotten eggs.

I dread Monday, but it comes anyway. It's easy to avoid Emily during business tech, since we don't sit by each other anymore, but at lunch, I slide my hair forward, unable to bring myself to look at her.

You know how they say the crook always returns to the scene of the crime? Well, if you ever become a criminal, I can tell you right now you should stay as far away as you can. Cynthia natters on, but Emily's quiet. My conscience pecks at my soul, saying, *Tell her what you did! Tell her what you did!* It sounds like a parrot. I cram my peanut butter sandwich into my mouth; it's the only way to keep words of confession from leaping off my tongue.

I peek at Emily, and her eyes flick away. I slide my Rice Krispies bar across the table, but she ignores it.

Cynthia makes a move for the treat. "Can I have it?"

I nod. For once, I'm glad Cynthia talks with her mouth open because her chatter makes this lunch period feel almost normal.

Emily didn't take my dessert, but I promised myself I would be extra nice to her to make up for the egg-throwing. When we're done eating, I try to take her empty milk carton to throw it out for her.

Her hand moves lightning fast, clutching the plastic container with superhuman strength.

"Oh, I'll get it for you," I say in my best waitress voice. "I've got to throw out my stuff anyway."

Pulling the carton closer to her side of the table, she picks at her raisins without eating them.

Cynthia offers me her used-up hot lunch tray, gross, half-eaten chicken strips with ketchup bloodying the stumps. I tell her to take care of it herself, then I clear my stuff, throw out my trash, and say good-bye as the bell rings. Emily turns her head in the opposite direction.

I don't know how I'm supposed to do good deeds for her when she's in such a weird mood.

★　★　★

In history, Mrs. Fuller talks about the St. Augustine field trip. We are to divide ourselves into groups of three or four, and a chaperone will be assigned to each group. She passes out questionnaires that we all have to fill out to show we've visited the assigned places. I try to become invisible as my classmates' happy voices chirp in the air, shouting for this person or that person to be in their group.

"Hailee!" Nikki shouts. She waves the sign-up sheet. "I've got you!"

My stomach churns.

After class, Nikki waits for me as I pick up my pencil, slide it into the outside pouch of my backpack. I pick up the St. Augustine papers and straighten them by knocking the edges against my desk. I smooth the bent corners of my workbook; I wish I'd been more careful with it because it looks damaged now.

Nikki doesn't notice how long I'm taking. Or maybe she doesn't mind. I sling my backpack on and listen as she tells me which boutiques she wants to show me in St. Augustine.

Why do you like me? I want to ask her. *Why are we friends?*

Outside, Alexis sidles up to Nikki's other side. She groans when Nikki mentions the field trip. "It's too hot," Alexis says. "I hate all those old buildings. We've already seen them, anyway."

I haven't. Nikki stops under the shade of an oak. She brings up the cool shops, but Alexis interrupts her by talking about the egg throwing as if it were an Olympic event and she won the gold medal.

I grab a low branch, hoist myself up, and perch amid the leaves.

"What are you doing?" Alexis's voice is a whine in my ears. Her face scrunches like it did when Libby pooped in her diaper.

This tree has good branches; I move up like I'm climbing a ladder.

Alexis leans toward Nikki. "Does she think she's a gorilla?"

I sit and stare down at them through the twigs. Nikki watches me. Alexis huffs like a bull and shrugs her shoulders. Their parts cut white lines through their heads.

"What do you see up there?" Nikki calls.

"Alexis's dandruff."

"I don't have dandruff!" She glides one hand over her hair.

I drop an acorn on her.

"Hey!"

The next one hits her forehead.

Almost all of her straight white teeth show as she curls her lips back like a chimpanzee. "Stop it!"

"Nine left," I say and shoot another one.

She raises her backpack over her head. "Come on," she says to Nikki, who tilts her face up at me. "Let's go."

I toss an acorn to Nikki and she catches it.

I stare at her and she stares at me, and then I grip the branch, turn, and climb down, twisted sprigs snagging my backpack and scratching my legs. Swinging off the bottom branch, I nail my landing and raise my eyebrows. "Should we go now?"

"Hang on," Nikki says. She raises a hand to me and I flinch, but all she does is brush off the top of my hair. A leaf flutters down beside me. "Let's go."

Alexis fiddles with her collar, flicking off acorns that aren't even there. To me, she says, "You're so weird."

"Shut up," Nikki says. It's the same voice she used on Jordan.

★   ★   ★

My head is swollen with thoughts of this past weekend and the uncomfortable way I felt at school. When I get home, my brain is bigger and heavier than my body. I lay my head on the table as Mom brings a snack along with her coffee.

"Mom?" I don't open my eyes. "What if you accidentally hurt someone and you didn't mean to and it wasn't your fault?"

I sense her lean forward with attention. "Someone got hurt?"

"Not like a broken leg or anything. But—"

"Hurt their feelings?"

I think about that. "No, not their feelings, just . . . never mind." There's no way I can tell her about the eggs.

She tries to pry more information out of me, but I put on the tired act so well she finally leaves me alone. "Maybe some fresh air would perk you up," she says. "You've been indoors ever since your party."

I trudge outside. My bike feels like too much work so I drag my feet along. I have to look down, the sun is so bright. My hair follicles burn like hot little pins in my head, and I slog through the humidity as if it's quicksand. This is not fresh air. I feel worse than before and I need relief.

I press Emily DeCamp's doorbell. As I wait, I slide my eyes left and right, looking for egg evidence, but it's all been washed away.

After a few moments, Emily cracks open the door, just a slice. A dull surprise blooms on her face, but she doesn't say anything.

"Hi," I say.

She waits.

I shift from foot to foot and shrug. "Just thought I'd come over and visit."

She presses her face against the narrow opening she's allowed. "I saw you."

Alarm streaks through my body. "What?"

Shaking her hair off her face, she repeats herself. "I saw you throwing eggs at my house with Nikki and Alexis." She says this flatly, in a monotone, a straight charcoal-colored line from her to me.

I don't know how to react. It would be easier if she were angry or laughing it off or something that would tell me what I should do next. Nikki launched my arm. That's the truth.

"It wasn't—" But I cut myself off. It *was* my fault. It was my eggs, my guests, and my party. I didn't do anything to stop it.

"I'm sorry," I say.

Her eyes well up.

Mine water in response. "I am so sorry."

"I don't know if I can forgive you right now." A tear slips under her glasses and she quietly shuts the door on me.

★   ★   ★

The next day, I hide by the cafeteria loading dock during lunch. As we head into history class, Nikki asks me about pitching those acorns.

"I don't know." Which isn't true. I do know; I just don't want to tell her.

She glances down, then leans her head and says, "Sometimes, I go into my mother's room and break her cigarettes. Then I put them back in the pack."

"Why?"

"I feel mad at her a lot."

"How come?"

"I don't know," Nikki says. I picture her sneaking into her mom's room, padding across the floor so she doesn't make a sound. Shadows slide over the walls. Even though blinds hung in every downstairs window I saw, in my version, long, sheer drapes billow mysteriously, carried by a wind that whistles through the house. Nikki pulls each slender white cigarette from the box and snaps it in half, carefully sticking each one back so her mom can't tell they're broken.

She's not so much older than I am.

I say, "I know what you mean." Then I take a chance. "I didn't like egging Emily's house."

She nods, the slow kind of nodding that's loaded with thoughts. "Sorry about that."

A kind of appreciation passes between us. My brain can't put words to it, but my heart understands it completely. I take my seat. I'm ready for this day to be over. If I were the sun, I'd call it a night.

Here's how my week goes: Each day I eat lunch alone

by the stinky Dumpsters. I do all my homework and all my chores without being asked, mainly because Amanda and Emily are mad at me and I can't text or get on Facebook. I take the Silver Flash out for a spin, but I have to ride in the opposite direction, away from Emily's house and nowhere near Amanda's.

Some kid blows out his trumpet lessons; the notes bleat loudly, so off-key, it would be a good deed to tell him he would probably make a really good accountant or librarian or some other quiet job.

Bright red roses splash against a deep green lawn. Their powdery smell says, *It's a pretty day*, but they lie because all roses have thorns. Why did God make something beautiful that can also prick your finger and make you bleed? Do you ever wonder about stuff like that? I do. Then I start thinking about why did he make cactuses prickly when desert animals need the water inside. Why do cherries have pits—you could choke on those, you know. And that would be the pits.

If I had my phone and could post that, I would add LOL.

Thursday, Mrs. Fuller goes over the field trip again. Some of the girls chatter about the cool shops and the stuff they've bought there before. My group will be chaperoned by Mrs. Grant, Gia's mother.

Mom's good mood when I get home makes me feel

even worse. I push away my snack and she doesn't even notice.

"You aren't the only person in a new school," she says brightly, handing just-woke-up Libby her sippy cup. Mom waves an envelope. "I've been accepted to the community college!"

I snap straight up. "College? Who's going to be here when I get home? Who's going to cook supper?" My baby sister makes noises, too, so I do the asking for her. "Who's going to take care of Libby?"

"Daddy will. You know he sets his own hours." Mom's smile radiates a hundred watts. "I'm going to college!"

"Why?" Why would a grown woman volunteer to go to school?

"Hailee," Mom starts, "I want to make something of myself."

"But you're a mom. You don't need to go to college."

Her face gets all serious. "Yes, I do. I *do* need to go to college."

"But why?"

"Because"—she softly brushes my cheek with her fingertips—"I need to."

All my life, when I came home from school, my mom was there. Now I'll have no one. I really am like Opal now, except no dog to make me feel better and no old lady friend who lets me have a party at her house.

I pull myself up like a bag of bones and drop myself upstairs on my bed. I don't even have a book to read because I finished *Because of Winn-Dixie* last night.

My cheery maple waves to me, but I turn aside and cry.

Chapter 30

. . . .

"In your groups, everyone! Sit with your group on the bus," one of the teachers yells.

The sun has barely opened its eyes and mine should still be closed, but here we are, six thirty in the morning, boarding the buses for St. Augustine from the school parking lot. Alexis spies me approaching and narrows her eyes. As our group pushes up to the bus door, she bumps me out of the way with her backpack and slips into a seat with Nikki. She doesn't care that her backpack nearly took my head off; in fact, she'd probably love that. If my mom's van was still here, I'd run right off this bus. I wouldn't care what people thought. I do not want to be on this field trip with that girl.

But I have to.

I climb aboard the bus like a sentenced prisoner. Gia, the fourth girl in our group—the girl who skipped school with Nikki and Alexis—pairs up with a friend, and I end up sitting next to her mother, Mrs. Grant. While everyone else chats with their seatmates, I lean my head against the window and try to sleep.

Not far out of town, a traffic accident plugs up the highway and we sit and we sit and we sit. After a while, the driver turns off the motor and the air conditioner. Everyone groans, but he explains he's got to conserve for the rest of the trip.

The bus becomes a hot tin can. The smell of armpits and sweat sours the air. Girls stand up and fan themselves, only to get yelled at by adults, who then get up and do the same thing. Nikki and Alexis entertain themselves with their phones. My only entertainment is smelling the ripe odor of other human beings and eating part of my lunch.

When the bus finally starts moving, roars and applause fill the air. Because we've lost so much time, the teachers are in a huge rush when we dismount in St. Augustine. Skip the Old Jail, they tell the chaperones, and the lighthouse, and the Oldest House. Don't worry about the questionnaires. Instead, we're going to two history museums, the Oldest Wooden Schoolhouse, and the Castillo de San Marcos National Monument, which is the old fort the Spanish built in the sixteen hundreds to protect themselves.

Some girls stretch their arms and arch their backs as we organize on the sidewalk. I do twenty-five jumping jacks. My bones can't take all that sitting around. Alexis snorts and points me out to Nikki. I don't care. I prance and fake a couple of boxing jabs in her direction. *Take that!* my fists say.

The fort is the coolest place ever. A real drawbridge lies over a real moat. Heavy chains hold it in place with big huge bolts. Clip-clopping over the planks, I look down. The moat is grass, and a guide tells us it always was—that's where the people in the fort kept their livestock. That's not how you're supposed to use moats! What did they think—the enemy would charge over the berm and be scared away by MooMoo the Moat Cow?

Staring down, I stir up a different picture for myself. Water the color of iced tea fills the moat, and water moccasins zigzag across the surface. Giant alligators shoot from its depths, crushing anything that drops into their powerful jaws of death. Poisonous seaweed grows in the water and if it touches you, you die a horrible instant death.

Now *that* is a much better moat. Probably I should write it all down and send it to their mayor in case he'd like to use it.

We're ushered down a stone staircase and into a large room hollowed out in the wall. For as hot as it is outside, the cavelike space is surprisingly cool. Air funnels down and breezes over us. A small, high window provides the only light. Long, wooden platforms with floppy pillows run along each wall. The Spanish soldiers slept here, the guide tells us, and the thin pillows are sacks filled with animal hair or hay that served as their mattresses. I try to imagine being so far from home, waiting to be attacked. Did the soldiers actually sleep on these sacks, or did they lie awake staring out the window at the moon, wishing they were home?

Nikki and Alexis hang back, while I stick with Gia and her mom. Bits of another school group surround us and we get caught in their tour. The guide says the whole fort is made of shells called coquina. I brush my hand against the wall.

"Don't do that," the guide snaps. She singles me out from the group with her pointy nose and her stern gaze. "This material is very old and can crumble. Please, don't anyone touch the walls."

Well! A fort that held off cannon fire and pirates but can't take one girl touching it. I did not know a fort could be of such delicate nature. When we peek in the barracks and the ammunitions room, I make a big point of keeping my arms rigid at my sides. I even walk like that.

The guide explains how the Spanish fought from the fort only when threatened, but later the British captured it and had to live inside its walls. Other girls press against the wooden rails to get a closer glimpse of the British quarters, but I move like a robot with no arms.

Mrs. Grant whispers, "I think it's okay if you relax. She didn't want you touching the walls because if everyone who comes here touches them, we'd wear it down."

I like walking like an alien.

We trump up the stairs, hugging the side because another tour group is coming down at the same time. It's even gustier up here. Mrs. Grant tries to hold her hairstyle in place with her hands, but I let my hair whip across my face. Cannons, real cannons, aim through cut-out areas, ready to blast the enemy. The rocky, uneven wall barely comes up to my waist. I peer over the edge and wonder if the blue-green river was this pretty hundreds of years ago.

Pulling strands of hair out of my mouth, I turn around and spot Nikki sneaking down the stairs. Alexis leans against the cannons on the middle of the roof, turned green by the sea air.

"What a beautiful background," Mrs. Grant says. "Girls, line up by the edge and let me take your picture." She turns around and calls to Nikki in a way that tells me she somehow sensed Nikki slipping away. "Come back, we're going to take a picture."

Nikki gives Mrs. Grant an exaggerated grimace and asks, "Do you mind if I run to the bathroom? I'll be right back."

Mrs. Grant thinks it's a great idea. "Let's all go," she says. "But first let's take this picture."

Nikki frowns. When she sees me looking, she pantomimes smoking a cigarette. I glance away quickly.

The sun broils my freckles and makes my shirt damp. After we use the bathroom, Mrs. Grant sprays Gia and me with sunblock. "Because you're so fair," she says.

Alexis sniggers.

After the fort, we walk to some of the small museums, then eat our lunches on a bench where I fry like a tomato. I'm as crisp as bacon and greasy from sunblock. Miserable.

Mrs. Grant checks her phone. "Oh! We have to be back on the bus in a little while. What do you girls want to do—hit the shops or visit the Oldest Wooden Schoolhouse?"

"Shop!" we all shout.

I am excited about the shopping. Never before have I been given money for anything besides food on field trips. But I'm loaded today. Who knows what I will buy? The sky's the limit.

Consulting the map, Mrs. Grant leads us to the shopping district. Fudge shops, candy stores, and ice cream parlors are too many to count. One shop is fashioned like a jewelry counter with different types of fudge filling the display cases: peanut butter, chocolate, coffee, maple, butterscotch, praline, vanilla, vanilla butternut, and more.

Everyone in our group buys fudge except for me. I can get chocolate any old time—I'm saving my money for something special. Near the fudge shop is a store with tie-dyed T-shirts hanging in the window. Nikki insists she will die if we don't go in. She and Alexis come out wearing dangling feather earrings.

Cotton candy, caramel corn, lattes—the other girls spend money as if they have ATMs in their backpacks. I watch them pay a ridiculous amount for strawberry lemonade as I sip from the bottled water I bought a couple stores ago. Mrs. Grant isn't any better. Bags and bags loop over her arms.

Finally, we stop in a boutique that has things I like. Barrels of gag gifts like black glasses with big noses and mustaches sit by the front door. I put one on. "Gia," I say.

Alexis scrunches her nose. "That's disgusting. You're probably breathing in someone else's mucus."

Mucus. So gross. I whip the glasses off and toss them in the barrel. Alexis looks at me as if I'm one giant snot.

"Where's Nikki?" Mrs. Grant says, glancing around from the postcard stand. Looking straight at Alexis, "Where is Nikki?"

Alexis makes big doe eyes. "I don't know," she says. "I'm sure she'll be right back, wherever she is."

Mrs. Grant scans the shop. "Gia?"

Gia puts down a wooden flute. "I don't know, Mom."

"Stay here, girls." Mrs. Grant makes a sweep through the store, then steps outside.

I look at Alexis as she watches out the window. Her

fake innocent eyes didn't fool me—she knows exactly what's going on. Then she suddenly pretends to be interested in the plastic snakes in front of her.

Glancing out of the window, I see Mrs. Grant walking with Nikki from behind the shop. Smoke curls from Mrs. Grant's hands. It takes me a second to realize she's caught Nikki in the act of smoking. I'm stunned. I can't look anywhere else. Mrs. Grant grinds out the cigarette in a potted plant and grabs Nikki by the elbow as they duck into the open doorway.

"Gia?" she commands. "You girls have ten more minutes to shop. Mrs. Fuller's waiting for Nikki and I'm escorting her to the drop-off. Just meet me there, okay?" She sounds like my mom on her worst day.

Nikki closes her eyes and sighs, like this is just one more thing on a very long and hard list.

Alexis says to Gia, "Is your mom always like that?"

Gia huffs, dismissing her own mother in one derisive snort.

I feel bad for Nikki, but at the same time, she shouldn't have been smoking. She should never be smoking. She should never be skipping; she should never be swearing; and she should never, ever ride in the backseats of cars driven by reckless boys she doesn't even know.

I close my eyes and sigh, too. I hope things turn out for her, but I have a feeling they won't.

Since this is probably the last store we'll visit, I decide

to concentrate on finding something good here. None of the St. Augustine mugs appeal to me, and neither do the silk-screened T-shirts. I pick up a rubbery clear ball that has a lighthouse inside. It bounces pretty well. I bounce it a few times, then catch it, and drop it back where I found it. I can collect my own shells, so I pass by entire shelves of them.

"Hey," Alexis says. "You got any money left?"

Trouble, a little voice in my head says. Alarms light up in nerves up and down my arms. "Well . . . yeah."

"Gimme some. I want to buy that hat."

"No!" I gulp. I feel like I used to every morning in the bicycle pen at Palm Middle. "I'm looking for something for someone."

"I know you've got at least two twenties. I saw them in your backpack when you got your lunch out."

I shake my head. My heart pings against my chest. I back off, but she closes in on me. Grown-ups are never around when you need them.

"Stop," I say. "Leave me alone."

She sneers. "Or what?"

"Or . . ." I gasp for air. "Or . . ." Then I take one huge balloon breath and let it slowly deflate from every single cell in my body. I am so tired of mean girls. "Leave me alone," I say, "or I will *finish* you." I tremble with rage and shake my jowls like the baseball coach. "I will SHUT YOU DOWN!"

"You little—" She jerks my arm.

I kick her in the shin. She yelps like a dog, crouches, then limps toward me.

I kick her in the other shin. Harder.

When she looks up, her eyes fill with angry tears. "You're so pathetic."

Pathetic feels pretty good as I watch her hobble away from me. My heart is still racing, but it feels strong. My toes hurt only a little bit; good thing they told us to wear sneakers for this field trip. *I will shut you down. Jerk. Kick.* Oh, my gosh! Wait till Amanda hears about this!

Then I remember my last words to her.

From the far corner near the door, Alexis complains to Gia so loudly, I can't help but hear her. She's talking about me, and you know what? I don't even care. I move deeper into the store and farther away from them.

The jewelry sparkles for my attention. Thin slivers of shiny beach shells, iridescent in creams and pinks, hang from leather chains. Turquoise rings remind me of the river I'd seen earlier. Then I spot a tiny compass on a golden rope necklace. Catching it in my hand, I move it in different directions. The hand inside spins.

This is perfect.

I'm so happy when the cashier hands me my bag. I turn around for Alexis and Gia, but they're not there. I coast between the shelves. "Alexis? Gia?" I call out. "Alexis?"

"Alexis!" I wait. "Alexis!"

I run out of the store and look left and right. I don't

see anyone I know. I don't see any blue Magnolia uniforms. I don't know which way we came from.

"Alexis!" I shout. My heart pounds like a bass drum.
Panic tightens my skin. Left or right, left or right? It all
looks the same to me.

I'm lost.

Chapter 31

. . . .

I pound the streets. I avoid all eye contact with strangers. My heart is racing and so are my feet. People mill around slow as turtles. *Get out of my way!* I have to find my bus. The shops and their wares look familiar and the same as each other. Rows of small buildings line both sides of the narrow streets. I break into a run.

Never talk to strangers. Don't look like a tourist. Act like you know where you're going.

A guy wearing sagging jeans and an open plaid shirt jogs alongside me. I cast a furtive look at him—unshaven, tan, and creased like old leather. My heart skips a frightened beat when his mouth slithers into a smile. "Where you in such a hurry to?"

I bolt from him. Run blind through alleys. Cross streets without looking. A car screeches to a stop, blares its horn at me. I run and I run and I run. My pulse shoots through my limbs. My hands feel swollen; my tongue is thick. Black dots dance across my vision and a rush of light-headedness overwhelms me to the point that I stumble up a curb, lean against a wall, and slide down.

Tremors quake inside me and burst through in shivers and shakes. I draw my knees up, wrap my arms around them, and burst into tears. I can't stop trembling.

"Excuse me—"

I look up. My face is wet. My skin is hot. "NO!" I growl.

A lady, a grandma lady. Taken aback as if I bit her.

I roll to my feet and though I back away, I bare my teeth. The hair on the back of my neck rises. I lower my head and sway, watching her, checking her movements.

She speaks gently. "I'm not going to hurt you. Are you okay? Do you need help?" Her face matches her voice, kind and concerned.

Keeping her at bay, I glance around. I don't recognize anything. The bus has left without me; this I know. Over and over this morning, they warned us to be on time or be left behind. A lump forms like a rock in my throat. I swallow and swallow again.

She takes a step forward.

"No!" I crouch into a defensive position. My mind races in total blankness. Tears dribble from my eyes. I can't stop swallowing.

"Okay," she says. She smells like chocolate chip cookies. Talking slowly and quietly, she says, "I'm going inside and I'll bring you something to drink, okay? Just stay right there."

My mouth quivers uncontrollably. I press my hands to my face.

The door cranks open. "I didn't know what you liked, so I grabbed a bottled water."

I don't answer.

She sets it down beside me and backs up.

"My name is Sylvia Stiles. I have three grown children and seven grandchildren, two of them girls. One is in fifth grade." She pauses—my cue to say something, but I don't.

"You'd like her. Her name's Molly. What's yours?"

I open the bottled water and chug it down so fast, I'm breathless when I stop. "I'm not supposed to talk to strangers." My voice comes out garbled. I swipe at my eyes. I could run past her if I needed to. She's old. She couldn't catch me.

Sylvia Stiles bites her lip. Her gray hair is longer than most old ladies wear it, and a braid hides under one side. "That's a good rule. Molly's mother has the same rule for her. But if Molly were lost, I hope someone nice would take a chance and help her."

She takes one careful step forward. Then another.

I crumple into tears.

Chapter 32

. . . .

My throat is clogged and Mrs. Stiles can't understand
what I'm saying. I let her lead me through her knick-
knack shop to a cozy little room with a wicker love seat
and a rocking chair. Her hands flutter around me, unsure
of themselves, and then she decides it's okay to hug me
and it's just what I need. The floodgates open. I cry about
missing the bus. I cry about Amanda. I cry about being
lost. I picture Mom and Dad—their faces when they
realize I'm missing—and I cry even harder.

Mrs. Stiles rocks me and talks about Molly. After a
while, I find myself listening and my tears slow down to
a trickle. I sniff up my blubbery snot and my body shudders with the relief of draining a thousand tears.

"Well," Mrs. Stiles says. "I'll bet people are wondering where you are."

I slobbily nod.

Mrs. Stiles lifts a phone from the side table. It's the old-fashioned kind with a cord. She picks up the handset, then replaces it. "I guess I should know your name!"

My mouth is sticky from crying. "Hailee Richardson."

"That's so pretty," she says. Her blue eyes light up with kindness. "Are you with a school group?"

I start bawling again. "I want to call my mom." I don't know if Mrs. Stiles understands me or not, but she puts the phone in my lap and I dial my home number. No one answers. I hang up and dial again. Hang up, dial. Hang up, dial. Hang up. The bottom of my stomach falls out. "They're not home!"

"Don't cry. Don't cry." Mrs. Stiles tries to calm me. "Do they have cell phones?"

Yes! Call their cell phones. My index finger aims at the keypad, ready to jab out the numbers, and then I realize I don't know them. They were programmed into my cell phone; I never had to memorize them. My chest threatens to burst.

No home phone, no Mom phone, no Dad phone. My mind wrings its hands. Then it dawns on me that there is one number etched in my brain since forever.

With slow, deliberate movements, I dial Amanda's house.

Chapter 33

· · · · · · · · · · · · · · · ·

Mrs. Stiles handles everything from there. She calls around the shops and before long, Mrs. Grant appears in the doorway looking as limp as unstarched laundry. The other girls had told her I'd left before them for the bus. When the teachers did a head count, they discovered they were minus one Hailee Richardson. Mrs. Grant waved the bus off and pounded doors and the pavement looking for me until she came upon a store manager who'd just received Mrs. Stiles's alert. "Thank God you're all right," Mrs. Grant says, looking as wiped out as I feel. Then she takes Mrs. Stiles's hand in both of hers. "Thank you."

Mrs. Stiles takes care of her, too, and we're all sitting in the back room a couple hours later when the shop door chimes, signaling someone has wandered in.

"Hello?"

Amanda's mom! I pop off the love seat, dart through the shop, and launch myself into Mrs. Burns's arms. She hugs me and pats my back, and it's almost as good as having my own mom's arms wrapped around me.

I lift my head and start to rattle off my tale of woe. Then I spot Amanda in the doorway, crossed arms, mad eyes.

"I'm so sorry," I say, looking at Mrs. Burns. "I'm sorry you had to drive all the way out here to get me." I glance at Amanda. "I'm sorry."

I hang my head and one big fat tear plops onto the floor, leaving a round wet spot.

"Oh, honey," Mrs. Burns says. "We're just glad you're okay. I couldn't get ahold of your parents, but I left them a message and a note on the front door."

Amanda and I don't look at each other as the adults chitchat for a few minutes. I hug Mrs. Stiles good-bye, then I'm in the backseat with Amanda heading home. Her mom and Mrs. Grant gab in the front while Amanda and I sit in stony silence.

I try to ignore the quiet between us, but it's too loud. It fills my ears and breaks my heart. I can't believe I have any tears left, but here they come. I cover my eyes with my left hand. Sobbing, I hunch over like a baby curling in her sleep.

"Hailee," Amanda murmurs and leans closer.

All the salt from tears and sweat have made my face sticky. I wipe my nose with my bare arm, then face her.

She starts crying. "Something could've happened to you!"

I start crying again. "I know!"

We cry together for a few minutes, then laugh at our crying, which makes us cry and laugh again.

Rubbing both eyes, Amanda looks straight at me. It's getting dark, but I can still see her. She starts to say something, changes her mind, then changes it again and says, "I was so mad at you. It was like . . . you were getting stuck-up just because you're so rich and popular now. And you were sort of mean to me at Emily's sleepover."

I think of how embarrassed I was at Emily's party—embarrassed of Amanda's clothes and embarrassed of Amanda's conversation—and then I see myself acting like I was *all that*.

Then Amanda says, *"And* you called me a—" She cuts herself off. "Well, you know what you called me," she says.

Witch with a B.

I hear myself saying those words and I cringe. The sharp tip of my poisonous words pierces my heart. They must still hurt Amanda, too, because she straightens away from me.

Silence sits between us on the seat, laughing at how it separates us.

I am guilty as charged. My crimes are many and

some are secret, but there's one person who knows about all of them. In my head, I ask God to forgive me for Happy Hannah Hearts, eggs, and witch with a B. I *don't* ask him to forgive me for kicking Alexis in the shins; the Bible says God loves justice, so you know he had to love that.

Mom says forgiveness is divine, but Amanda is human and she doesn't have to forgive me. I wouldn't forgive me.

I feel like I did when I egged Emily's house, only this time, I will try to clean up the mess I made. "I'm sorry."

She doesn't move or say anything.

She's still my best friend. If you don't believe that, then just ask yourself why is she in this car right now? It's like a two- or three-hour trip from Palm Hill; she didn't have to come, but she did. Don't worry if you didn't see that right away—I just realized it myself.

"You are the best friend a person could ever have," I say. "I'm the witch, not you."

She looks down, then purses her lips. "You're not a witch."

"Neither are you." My hands clasp in my lap and I look down. "Guess what else? I'm not popular. I just wanted you to think I was. Plus"—and I try to keep the hurt out of my voice—"you have a boyfriend now and you asked him to do your last project with you. I thought you and I were going to do them together."

Her mouth parts. "But you've been busy with Library Club."

"You've been busy with Tanner."

"Why didn't you want me at your sleepover?"

Taking a deep breath, I exhale. There's so much to explain and I am so tired. The windows darken as the highway takes us closer and closer to home. I open my bag and give the little jewelry box to Amanda.

Her hand covers her heart. "For me?"

"I told them I was looking for something special."

She flips on the side light, then opens the box. "Told who? It's so pretty! It's a compass—oh, my gosh—it's a compass, for the Compass Club! I love it!" She hugs me hard, then fastens the chain around her neck. She tilts the compass and reads it. "We're heading *south*," she says emphatically. "South, Mom—got it?"

"Oh, thank you," Mrs. Burns says. "Now I have a GPS."

In a robotic voice, Amanda says, "Take next exit for McDonald's."

"Go through drive-through. Buy milk shakes." I speak and move my arms like an automaton. "Use apparatus known as straw to drain container of substance."

Amanda jerks her arms, lifts her robot voice to her mother. "Milk shakes. Buy some. McDonald's in point-five miles."

"Point five," I drone.

"Milk shakes," Amanda orders.

"Oh, my gosh, girls!" Mrs. Burns says. "I'm going to buy milk shakes just to hush you two up."

We break into android laughter. Ten minutes later, Mrs. Burns has her wish and so do we.

Chapter 34

· · · · · · · · · · · · · · ·

I get two yearbooks at the end of the school year: Palm Middle, which I ordered way back in October; and Magnolia, where I'll be attending through eighth grade. Amanda passed around my Palm Middle yearbook and had everyone sign it, but her autograph is my favorite. On the page with her photo, she's written along the gutter where the pages are glued in:

> *I signed your crack! Ha-ha! Hailee, you are my best friend always and we are going to have the most awesome summer!*
>
> *Amanda*

Magnolia's yearbook is beautiful. Lying on my stomach on my bed, I pore over the faces of the friends I've made this year and read what they've written.

We should hang out this summer!
Cynthia

One of my best students!
Ms. Reilly

Have a great summer and keep reading!
Hope to see you in Library Club next year.
Mrs. Weston

I wasn't able to get Nikki's signature because her parents took her out early for a trip to Europe. Next year, she's going to boarding school. I hope she doesn't get herself into any more trouble.

Ever since St. Augustine, I've been trying to think about what makes Nikki different from girls like Alexis or Megan. I mean, they're all pretty and they're all popular, but I think it boils down to this: Nikki has her own problems, but she's still nice to people. The other girls are mean because they *can* be mean and they *want* to be mean and it makes them feel good to make others feel bad.

In my opinion, that's the worst crime a citizen can commit.

And just so you know, Alexis and Gia got in trouble for causing Mrs. Grant and me to be left behind in St.

Augustine. Not only did they get in-school suspensions, they had to write apology letters to me, my parents, Mrs. Grant, and Mrs. Burns.

I sigh into my Magnolia yearbook.

I want so much for Emily's signature to be on these pages. Flipping over to the sixth graders, I find her student photo. The photographer must have asked her to move her hair off her face. She's smiling in the picture, like we all do—smiling because we're told to, smiling because we're nervous, and smiling because we hope our pictures will turn out well and people, when they look at us later, will point to us and say, *Remember her? She was really nice.*

Emily and I haven't talked since the day she shut the door on me.

But I remember her. She was really nice.

Tucking the yearbook under my arm, I jog downstairs. Happy Hannah Hearts sits in the saucer while Libby bangs the musical buttons. I ruffle Libby's hair, then give Mom a peck on the cheek as she reads the course catalog from the university.

Dad's been teasing her about being a *co-ed*, whatever that means. I'm kind of proud of her, too. It takes a lot of guts to start a new school. Mom lowers the catalog and looks over her reading glasses. "Where you off to?"

"Just around," I say. "On my bike."

The Silver Flash and I make it to the perfect green grass in record time. From her window, Emily's flute trills like a bird in summer. I listen for a few minutes, then swipe down my kickstand and walk up to the front door.

I rap my signature knock.

The flute stops.

I wait.

I press my face against the etched glass but I can't see through it.

I ring the doorbell.

Minutes pass.

Emily isn't ready to open the door.

That's okay. My friendship will wait for her. As I turn from her front door, I lay the yearbook down and break off a twig from the bushes. I snap it in two and arrange the halves into an X behind the banister.

★   ★   ★

When Dad comes home, we grill outside to celebrate the end of the school year. Dad flips burgers and turns the corn on the cob, but mostly he looks past the grill, smiling at the roof of the garage, where brilliant displays of bright pink bougainvillea explode like fireworks. Mom's blasting her favorite track on the CD player—a song called "Macarena." I'm blowing bubbles for Libby when my phone tweedles.

Amanda: Tanner kissed me after school today!

I nearly spill the bubbles. I cap the bottle and leap up.

Me: omg! OMG!

I shake my shoulders and move my hips. Mom catches sight of me, then sticks her right arm out and lifts her left leg. Then left arm out and right leg up. This is the dance for the song. Libby sees what we're doing and starts bouncing from her knees.

Amanda: Call me!

"Mom!" I roar. "I've gotta call Amanda!" Mom waves me off, keeps dancing with Libby.

I prance around the yard and punch in Amanda's number.

"Hello?" she answers breathlessly.

"It's me," I say. "Tell me everything."

LIST OF THINGS I NEED

1. New bicycle
2. Cell phone
3. New clothes (from where Megan and Drew shop)
4. Full-length mirror
5. TV for my room
6. DVD player for my TV
7. TV stand
8. New furniture for my room
9. ~~computer laptop~~
9. Computer
10. Laptop
11. ~~New backpack~~
11. ~~Chandeliers~~
11. Mansion
12. Butler

13. Horse
14. Yacht
15. Indoor pool
16. Home movie theater
17. **Nanny**
18. Limo
19. Credit card
20. A movie about a girl who wins the lottery and I star in it
21. Convert attic to a huge bedroom like Emily's and call it Hailee's Kingdom
22. Books, but I can put them on my credit card
23. Trampoline
24. Private jet
25. Tree house in backyard and Libby's <u>not allowed</u> in it
26. Chef
27. Cool sunglasses like Nikki's
28. Fancy water fountain in the front yard
29. New furniture and decorations for the whole house (no naked lady statues; make sure Mom knows)
30. Bodyguard
31. Disco ball
32. One of those beds that has a slide built onto it, probably bunk beds so Amanda doesn't have to sleep on the floor when she spends the night

33. Snow machine for in the winter
34. Make the president change Halley's Comet to Hailee's Comet
35. A telescope so I can see Hailee's Comet
36. Dog—cute, not too big
37. Maid (who also has to pick up the dog poop)

Acknowledgments

I am thankful to God for the gifts he gives and the ability to use and enjoy them.

Thank you to my group of young contributors who helped brainstorm ideas for Hailee's "List of Things I Need" and for their thoughts on the life of a sixth grader: Brooke Haworth, Zachary Haworth, Matthew Haworth, Allie Furnari, Caroline Furnari, Jack Bennett, and Alexandra Eugster. Also, thank you to Benton Wood, the most colorful and dynamic Little League coach I've seen since my own father commanded the dugout.

Ted Malawer, as always, and special thanks to Michelle Carr and Steve Haworth for reading the manuscript with great care and thought and giving me honest feedback.

I like to give my editor her own paragraph because I want her to know how much I appreciate her talent.

Stacy Cantor Abrams helps me write a better book. I am grateful to work with Stacy and all the people at Walker Books.

And I'm especially grateful to you—the reader—because here I am typing this and there you are reading this, and without you, none of us would be here.